HEROES OF AVALON - BOOK THREE

WAR OF THE GODS

HEROES OF AVALON - BOOK THREE

WAR OF THE GODS

CEARA COMEAU

ISBN 978-1-7335664-6-9 (Paperback Edition)
ISBN 978-1-7335664-7-6 (eBook Edition)

This novel is a work of fiction. Names, characters, events, incidents, and locations are products of the author's imagination. Certain mythological concepts, names, and objects are also mentioned, but their origins may or may not be imaginary.

Cover Design by Matthew Crafton
of Space Viking Productions

Published in 2025 by Ceara Comeau
www.booksistersproductions.com

IN PRINCIPIO
Part One

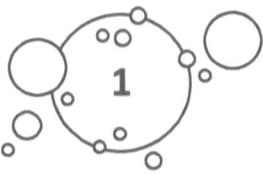

1

Two arms. Two legs. Ten fingers and ten toes. A cream-colored flesh stretched over his skeleton, revealing his thin new form. His sight wasn't as clear as before, but he could easily see he did not reach his destination. In fact, his transport appeared different. It took him a moment to realize he was standing on top of it. The vessel's solid, bumpy surface loomed before him. He was inside of it a solar cycle ago, floating around in his typical vapor form, or maybe it was longer. Time felt different in this new galaxy. The being tilted his head down and looked past his bare extremities. The familiar black smoke swirled around the violet-colored interior. His new face stared blankly into the colorful abyss, wondering how he could transform into a shape he had never been able to do before. *Power* was the only word that came to his mind, a power that his masters did not calculate for. It did not matter; this change did not affect his overall mission. But how? As he looked over the galaxy he landed in, he felt no lifeforms to speak of. He needed humans to continue the experiment. There weren't even earth-like beasts. There was nothing.

Suddenly, a brilliant light shot towards a far distant planet on the opposite side of the solar system. It landed with such a force that its light engulfed the sphere. Struggling, the being forced his sight back to what it once was and focused on the distant world. Laying on the planet's surface was another entity with features similar to his new form, although they were visibly different. It was what the humans of earth would identify as female, and according to their ways and opinions, they'd deem her appearance beautiful. However, the word meant very little to him. The creature rose to her feet and covered her naked body with a strange material, yet another custom he had little understanding of. She looked around at her new surroundings, and her lips curved upwards—a sign of contentment. Her energy felt familiar to him, as if he had passed her on his journey.

But he did. In his young memory, the being recalled a planet his vessel accidentally brushed against, knocking it out of orbit. When he set off from his home world, his mission had a targeted path. A minuscule solar system consisting of only four planets. His masters formulated the trajectory; it was flawless. So why did he not settle there? Perhaps the vessel had a mind of its own- after all, it was organic in nature. His thoughts returned to the present, and his focused sight stared at the newcomer, whose eyes were now seemingly fixed on him. His theory was correct. This was the soul of the planet he hit. The lines of hair above her eyes pinched downward. She felt rage.

His mission remained unchanged; his masters were still observing, but this variable was unprecedented. The mission would have to wait.

***

"Concede, Dullahan, there is no shame in that," said the woman.

The creature never understood why the being had to give him a name. It was pointless; humans named things they have an emotional attachment to, and for the life of him, the Dullahan couldn't understand what hers was to him. Hatred, perhaps, maybe even jealousy? Whatever the emotion, it was irrelevant. This was not the first time she confronted him, and definitely not the first time their conversation began with this statement. Like the name, this conversation was pretty pointless. For some unknown reason, the creature, who named herself Danu, was obsessed with being in control of the solar system. Although, she didn't have complete control. One of the first things Danu did when she arrived was reorganize the planets so they all surrounded her. That wasn't control—a mere decoration at best.

Danu crossed her arms in a challenging manner. But, the Dullahan found nothing challenging about it. Over the last millennia of their acquaintanceship, she failed to realize that he did not care about her desire for control. To her, his apathy translated as a desire for power as well. But he never explained himself to her, there was no need. She wouldn't understand his mission—no one would.

"I do not comprehend your meaning," he repeated for what seemed like the hundredth time.

"There cannot be two rulers in this solar system. You forced me from my home world, a world where I controlled everything."

The Dullahan looked at her, forming all sorts of responses in his mind. He could have stayed with the same words he had used repeatedly, but then the conversation would be even more of a waste of his time. Instead, he replied, "You only controlled your planet, not the solar system."

The thin lines of hair above her eyes pinched again, and her fingers wrapped tightly around her hands. She was feeling anger towards the Dullahan yet again. He always found this peculiar; whenever he pointed out a flaw in her thinking, she expressed this powerful emotion. She was almost exactly like humans but was not human; she was just a planet with human-like emotions. This concept was something the Dullahan couldn't process. What experiment could have caused this, and what was its purpose? Aside from his human form, why did he not gain these emotions? What was the chemical composition that made him and Danu so different? Just another scientific mystery to be solved at a later time.

"And what is wrong with controlling the solar system? What is wrong with being ambitious in my endeavors?" she asked, her voice getting an octave higher with each question.

"I do not know. Our missions are not the same."

"Then what *is* your mission?" she hissed.

"Your level of understanding would not comprehend it. Therefore, I will not explain."

"' My level of understanding?'" Danu gasped, "How dare you insult my intelligence!"

His comment finally made the enraged woman snap. A golden string of light materialized around her wrist, coiled around her hand, and grew to the ground. Before the Dullahan could understand the meaning of this new element, the woman flicked her wrist, and the bright light flashed across his face. His vision blurred briefly, and the world around him spun uncontrollably. Dirt was all he could see at first, but as his eyes turned up, he saw Danu standing over him with almost a maniacal grin on her face. She looked up toward where he once stood. The Dullahan looked at her in confusion as there was a glint in her eye followed by victorious laughter. Struggling, he turned his head to see his body was standing upright—his head cut clean off. Seeing he was still alive in every way, the Dullahan closed his eyes and focused his energy on a more familiar form. Within seconds, he felt his head return to his body, and his form was complete. Danu looked at him in disgust. She always seemed to dislike his original appearance. Although, it made no sense to him. His only conclusion was that he was more powerful in this state. Her glowing whip would have absolutely no effect on him. He already suspected his human form was a weak one to begin with, so his missing head did not matter to him. However, Danu's fast-growing strength was not expected. It would matter very little in the grand scheme of things, though.

He decided to let her have this moment of victory. In fact, he eventually decided it was best if she took credit for all the so-called "victories." After all, if Danu believed she was winning against him, she wouldn't be in his way. Of course, she wasn't winning at anything because it would require him to act against her. But whatever made her show up less in his domain was fine with him. With this plan in mind, he experienced what the humans of Earth might call peace. He was free to continue with his plan, scope out the surrounding planets, and integrate them into his grand scheme. While he sent little spies out to collect information, Danu went silent. No complaints, no attempts at making contact—nothing. Then, he heard a commotion coming from a planet near hers, and a brilliant light engulfed the planet. The Dullahan's eyes narrowed, focusing on this new anomaly. Something new was forming, and he wanted to see it. He quickly analyzed the situation and considered all the variables he may encounter. The only way to see this new formation closer without being caught by Danu was to change into a spatial specter- a form of his own invention. A tingling sensation wrapped around his natural form, and his feet slowly turned into particles.

Tiny black crystals inched their way up his body, erasing any memory of his figure.

When he was entirely transformed, the Dullahan shot off toward the planet, ensuring he would stay a few hundred thousand miles away. He found a comfortable spot to conceal himself as he watched the scene before him. Danu sauntered across the plane in search of something. *Perhaps she was not the cause of the anomaly?* The Dullahan thought, but his mind changed when she caught sight of a distant figure smelling blue flowers. Danu raised her dainty hands and cast a blinding light upon the figure, disorienting it. Quickly, she teleported herself right next to the figure, making her look like the deity she was trying to portray. The new creation was expectedly in awe at Danu's presence. He couldn't hear what was said, so he inched closer to the planet. Their voices were barely audible, and only a few words came through loudly and clearly. It was enough for him to know that Danu was trying to convince this creature, who she called Cerridwen, that she was created by her. The Dullahan was curious about Cerridwen's sudden need to please the female she named Mother. Cerridwen hadn't known Danu long enough to even give her a title, let alone one that had so much meaning.

This creature had strong emotions, much like Danu. However, she was of an entirely different world. A strong power emanated from her that matched Danu's, though that was the only resemblance. When Danu seemed confident that Cerridwen was under her control, she caressed her cheek in a motherly way and disappeared. The new mother reappeared again on the planet and out of sight of her child. She looked up toward the heavens and locked eyes with the Dullahan's spatial form. *Interesting. She believes I am watching her, and I am caught unaware. She has only altered her mission. This does not concern me, but knowing what she is doing with this life form might benefit me.*

A devious smile formed at the edges of her lips, and her left eyebrow arched. Her expression attempted to challenge the Dullahan, though he did not understand why. That familiar golden glow inched up her body, gradually transforming her. Her face was the last thing to vanish before her astral body launched into the air like the tail of a comet. Danu formed herself into an orb and floated high above her stolen planet. Within a blink, the solar system vibrated with all different colors—Danu and Cerridwen's planets were excluded. And just like the first two, it only lasted a split second.

Every planet now contains a life form that represents it, the Dullahan thought briefly. *I can use this to my advantage.*

After many solar cycles, Danu's creations started the next chapter in their evolution, the Dullahan scanned the galaxy for the most promising opportunity. The lightest planets were either too fixated on pleasing their false mother or creating lighter magic. It revolted the Dullahan. He turned his attention to some of the darker planets who were only self-absorbed. They would not be easily persuaded to join him. But then, there was this one planet in particular that he viewed as neither dark nor light. It was the God of Harvest. At least, that was what Danu titled him. He seemed to have his own way of doing things, which intrigued the Dullahan. This god, who called himself Dagda, ignored Danu's suggestions and reformed his planet as he believed it should be. He started by moving the lands around and dividing them into separate sections, which would produce different types of harvests. The one location that caught the Dullahan's attention was a peculiar mountain range with a narrow path separating them. Each part of the mountain range contained a rather large crater that could only be seen from the sky. These craters were home to hundreds, if not thousands, of hideous-looking beasts that could terrify any being. The Dullahan raised an eyebrow as he watched the creatures meander about.

Do it. The moment is most opportune, came the familiar voices in his head. They rarely spoke to him; when they did, it was only to reiterate what he already knew.

"I am aware," he replied calmly, "There are also other planets with other creatures. The moment might be opportune with this one, but it is not our only option."

Correct, but at this precise time, it is.

"Yes, Master."

After calculating every possible scenario he might face on the ground, the Dullahan changed his form in a breeze and turned into his familiar space dust. His form floated over his planet's horizon and smoothly flowed to his next target. As he broke through the atmosphere, he took in the planet's layout and noticed he was heading straight for a sea of green with every shade imaginable. Details quickly came into view, and with his advanced sight, he could see the branches and leaves of trees. He was landing in a forest that could consume most of planet Earth. His astral form neared the ground, and his feet began to take shape. The Dullahan looked around at the thick forest when his body became solid. Wind whipped through the treetops, and the sound of distant rivers echoed in his ears. The smell of wet dirt wafted into his nose as he walked through the endless forest. With his attention on the tree line around him, the Dullahan thought this location would be ideal for sending his enemies. They'd undoubtedly get lost or lose their mind. Fortunately, he knew exactly where he was going, or rather, who he was patiently waiting for. Any minute now, Dagda would sense a foreign presence in his world and would quickly appear. This was something most of Danu's *children* seemed to have in common—an insatiable curiosity.

The Dullahan reached a large clearing in the thick forest where dark green grass covered the ground. He stopped for a moment, analyzing his surroundings. The constant breeze grew into gusts of wind as a spiral of leaves emerged from the sky. It swirled around the clearing as if watching the foreigner—almost daring it to make the wrong move. The leaves finished their path in front of the Dullahan and increased their speed, creating a seven-foot tornado. It ended its windy dance by first revealing feet, then legs, a torso, and finally a head. And a stern expression came with the rugged face. The Dullahan had no appropriate description for this being. It appeared rougher than the others he had overseen, and judging by his clothing and earthy odor, Dagda didn't seem at all worried about what the other planets thought. His expression turned a bit softer, but now he appeared suspicious. The Dullahan stood his ground as Dagda started to walk the edge of the clearing, constantly watching the stranger.

"Who are you?"

Typical introduction. Why must it always be predictable? The Dullahan wondered, but he anticipated this response. He knew how this would end, "Who I am is of no consequence."

"I disagree," the Dagda said as he quickened his pace, "You must be of great importance to come to my humble world. I sense a magic surrounding you, though you do not originate from this solar system. So, I will ask again. Who are you?"

The god's tone had become dangerous, not that the Dullahan was worried. This was going according to plan, "Nothing."

"Well then, nothing; if you're not intruding for the sake of intrusion, then how can I help you?" the Dagda asked, completing a circle in front of the Dullahan.

"I need no assistance. But you do," the Dullahan cryptically replied. His human form remained rigid—almost neutral. "Your planet lacks the element of security. I can provide that."

Dagda's eyes narrowed, and his eyebrows furrowed. The Dullahan even noticed the faint grunt that escaped the god's partially opened mouth. *I have caused a negative response. Just as we suspected.*

"I do not need security unless you are under the impression my world will be conquered. If this is the case, I can easily prevent that if you tell me who you believe my enemy to be."

This creature is clever. I am impressed with our first choice of subject, "You have none, that is certain. This universe, however, is extensive, and you are eternal. The possibility exists that you might encounter a less-than-appealing individual. What I offer is merely a suggestion."

Dagda's eyes stared off into the deep forest, and nodded absentmindedly—taking in this stranger's words with sincerity. He took his gaze off his target, and his eyes returned to the Dullahan, "What did you have in mind?"

"This forest is a labyrinth for any creature with little intelligence. I have also determined that the gravitational pull of your planet will always bring celestial beings like myself to this forest first. However, I can find the exit to this forest, as will any other powerful being. You need a guard to ward off other entities who may arrive on your planet uninvited. Therefore, you would be alert to their presence and quickly identify if they are friend or foe before they exit the forest," the Dullahan explained simply.

The god walked toward the edge of the clearing and placed a hand on a pine tree. His mouth turned up in a faint smile, and he closed his eyes. As if trying to focus in on something— waiting for an answer to this stranger's suggestion. He then looked back to the Dullahan and replied, "Your point is valid, Nothing. I would like to hear more of your plan."

We have him! The Dullahan thought, satisfied that he didn't have to be deterred from his other ideas. He quickly played out the rest of the plan, contemplated every possible outcome, and replied, "Let us begin."

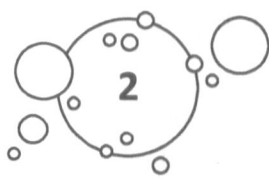

2

The female creature was stupid at best. But Dagda didn't seem to mind. He was more impressed that he created something with similar features to himself. *I could do that if I were unconscious, provided that that could happen to me,* the Dullahan thought. He watched Dagda fawn over his new creation—Rosemerta is what he called her. Objectively, her appearance was flawless and would attract any being. She flitted around the clearing and wove between the trees, giggling like a tiny human female. The Dullahan leaned against a nearby oak tree and crossed his arms, reflecting on the last few hours during which Rosemerta was created.

After persuading Dagda that he needed security, the god thought for a few minutes about what he deemed a good form of security. The Dullahan watched his movements as he grabbed a fistful of wind and combined it with several nearby branches and leaves. The branches were used as ligaments, hovering in place due to the constant airflow. With both hands and a big smile, Dagda instructed the dirt from the ground to spiral up with the movement of the wind—that formed her flesh. The leaves acted as the essential organs. Rosemerta's form was now solid. When Dagda was pleased with her appearance, he deeply inhaled and breathed on the female. This reminded the Dullahan of a particular individual in an Earth religion, but the name escaped him. With this last step, Rosemerta was born. The Dullahan couldn't understand this process. There was no method, scientific plan, or even a hypothesis—Dagda created her without thought.

His form of magic is not one I can compute. I must proceed with the next test, the Dullahan thought, pushing away from his station.

He approached Dagda's side and lifted his head, "That is a unique creature you made. How is she going to protect your land?"

Dagda continued watching Rosemerta, who began dancing to music only she could hear. The god chuckled and said, "Why, is it not obvious? She will create the perfect distraction."

"Go on," said the Dullahan, surprised the god managed to confuse him.

"As you said, this forest is not confusing enough to lose a deity. But Rosemerta was created to confuse them more. Any intruder would get irritated with her before they found the end of the forest," Dagda said proudly.

"That is clever, but this is only a portion of your world. What about the rest?" the Dullahan asked, glad the conversation was leaning in his direction.

Dagda's smile disappeared from his face and was replaced by a mask of concern. He looked through the trees around him as if peering into the rest of his world. He nodded silently, agreeing with the stranger's statement, "There is one location I often worry about. My fields. They have a fragile system, and any slight alteration could ruin everything."

"This sounds like something that certainly needs protection!" the Dullahan replied, trying to mimic emotions.

Dagda caught onto his facade and replied, "Yes, but I do not know how or what to do. You have powers. Would you like to assist?"

With a feigned smile and a false tone of excitement, the Dullahan replied, "Why, I would be honored!"

The two acquaintances magically vanished from the forest after Dagda bid his new creation farewell. This was a concept the Dullahan could not comprehend. She would live forever, and they would have plenty of time together. So why say goodbye? As the Dullahan silently ridiculed Dagda's behavior, the two quickly found themselves at the edge of the fields. He watched as the Harvest God walked in between the rows of plants. The Dullahan found this setup to be quite unusual but also literal. Each plant went through a harvest cycle, which soared into the sky as if it were on a wheel. Although it was creative, the Dullahan found no purpose in growing food in such a way. But he never ate, so his thoughts on the subject were insignificant. Dagda stared at the Dullahan—his expression revealing his uncertainty about the idea. The Dullahan silently gestured for the god to proceed, and a fake smile followed.

Dagda raised his massive arms, and with the flick of his fingers, every plant in the field sacrificed a tiny section of its roots. The god began waving his arms like a musical conductor and instructed the roots to congregate in one area. This was the Dullahan's chance. As the roots started to form a being, he joined Dagda and raised his hand toward the new creation. A smile formed on Dagda's face as he felt the powerful surge of magic. The Dullahan's ruse was working, and Dagda believed he was helping. That was furthest from the truth, though. The crafty being emitted energy, but the Dullahan wasn't helping or hindering the maker. In fact, he was trying to sense how Dagda's power worked. He would use this information later. The wooden creature turned into a shrub with a head full of greenery. There was absolutely nothing about this creation that indicated it was a guardian.

"And there it is! I call it a Bark Guard," the tall god replied, stifling a laugh, "It has bark, and it will guard. Is that not funny?"

The god let out a belly laugh that vibrated the ground beneath their feet. *At least he is satisfied with what he has done,* the Dullahan thought.

"It is quite a unique creation," the Dullahan lied, thinking of the similar shrubbery on Cerridwen's planet. "How do you intend for it to guard the fields?"

Dagda looked at the shrubs as they waddled around the garden aimlessly. He looked perplexed, as if he figured that creating them would automatically make them protect the garden from outside intruders. The Dullahan observed this reaction. The God of Harvest somehow believed that creating these shrub beasts would make them guard this portion of the world. Dagda had no understanding that he had to make his creations with intention. This perfectly explained to the Dullahan why Rosemerta was created with so little intelligence. Perhaps the concept of danger was so foreign to this god that it was barely a word to him. He had never experienced anything of the sort. The Dullahan could only wonder how Dagda would react to a threat of low impact.

"Disregard my previous question. These creatures are quite adequate in protecting your garden."

The god smiled at his new friend and moved forward, urging him to follow, "If you like these creatures, I guarantee you will like the next ones I have to show you. They dwell in a strange part of my world."

As the Dullahan followed the god, he discreetly looked back on the shrub creatures. As he moved, he lifted a hand and pointed at them as a silent stream of magic engulfed them. The Dullahan glanced back to Dagda, who began talking about the creatures he wanted to show his new friend—dinosaurs, he called them. Although the Dullahan made the appropriate vocal comments, he was not paying attention. He was fixated on what was becoming of the shrub creatures. Their green leaves wilted rapidly, leaving nothing but spindly twigs. Their bark looked slightly rotted, and a strange, thick substance oozed from the tips of the branches. It dropped on the ground, landing with a fizzing sound.

Excellent, I have deduced how his powers function. Therefore, my powers combined with his created precisely what I had expected. This test is now completed. Now, for the final test.

The Dullahan followed his guide through a vast, empty plain. A single pond stood in the center, and a mirror pond hovered over it. The clear waters were just as empty as the land. Far off in the distance stood a hut built into a nearby mountain. Dagda's facial expression appeared joyful. His face almost radiated light with how pleasant he seemed to feel. As he followed Dagda across the land, the Harvest God began regaling his new friend about his plans for this part of the world. The Dullahan only heard half the conversation—picking out the most essential information.

He planned for the land to become a home to another set of creatures. Dagda rattled off many names, which he would call them, though the Dullahan didn't catch all the titles. When he asked why they'd be set apart from the ones he would see, Dagda had an almost mischievous glint in his eye—as if he was waiting for that exact question. His only response was, "You will see soon."

The Dullahan was patient. He had nowhere to be but here. He feigned enthusiasm, and Dagda seemed to enjoy the suspense. Dagda continued on toward a large mountain, continuing his conversation about his plans. Still, he only stopped speaking when they reached the mountain base. It majestically towered above them, giving off an almost foreboding sense. At least, that would be how any other being might perceive it. The Dullahan watched as Dagda stared straight at the mountain wall, waiting for something to magically appear before him. The Dullahan looked to the left and right, wondering if a mechanism was supposed to trigger a doorway or a lift to bring them up and over the mountain. But even looking up gave him no results—low-hanging clouds were all that greeted him.

"Well, are you not coming?" Dagda asked, a smile stretched across his face.

"Please, after you."

Dagda shrugged and faced the mountainside. Effortlessly, he stepped forward and seemingly melted into the mountain. The Dullahan cautiously stepped forward—intrigue driving him. He reached out a hand and gently stroked the slab of rock that ate his guide. It felt foreign, unlike any rock he'd ever felt. It almost felt like vibrating water. Fingers emerged from the rock and snatched the Dullahan's wrist. Suddenly, he was pulled into the mountain as a wave of electricity seemed to encompass him. A blinding light surrounded him—a light that was even brighter than the sun from the barren fields he left behind. When his eyes adjusted, he saw Dagda standing before him. His face was beat red, and a smile stretched from ear to ear. He burst into a deep belly laugh, pleased with himself for the surprise he sprung on the Dullahan. But, the Dullahan wasn't surprised, and he most certainly didn't show it. This was yet another anomaly he was prepared for and one of no consequence. He let the god continue his laughter as he took in his surroundings.

He and Dagda stood in a small sphere whose edges shone brightly. With every belly laugh Dagda let out, the sphere moved along with his movements. The Dullahan looked at the walls of dirt surrounding them. This wasn't a cave or even a door of any kind. In fact, the dirt seemed to be pressing against the bubble everywhere. Tons and tons of dirt could have easily flattened them. Yet, somehow, this magical sphere protected them.

"Please explain this contraption," the Dullahan gestured.

"My mind controls this sphere," Dagda replied as he started moving forward. The dirt around him bending at his will, "As you can see, the dirt moves around us. There is really nothing to explain about it."

"Why not create a doorway? Would that not be simpler?"

"On the contrary, my creations would find a way onto the planes. As you will soon see, it could be catastrophic if they were loose."

Catastrophe was not a foreign word to the Dullahan. In fact, it seemed to follow him everywhere he went, though it was mostly by his choosing. The dirt wall gradually became rocky after a short walk from their entry point. Dagda stopped suddenly, and the mountain wall began to melt away, revealing a massive crater. Different shades of green blanketed the crater. An enormous lake stood in the center, acting as a watering hole for the unusual beasts that swarmed the edges. Sand and varying rocks lined the edges of the crater.

To the Dullahan, this volcano appeared to have elements that satisfied all the creatures. He looked up at the clear blue sky, and the corner of his lips turned up. This was the perfect testing ground.

"I see nothing catastrophic in this setting. These creatures appear harmless. In fact, let us release them for a short time. After all, it is your world, and you can easily rebuild it."

Dagda raised his hands in protestation but was too late. The Dullahan, knowing the workings of Dagda's magic, pointed a finger to the sky and fractured the invisible barrier around the volcano. The shield of protection shattered, its clear magic reflecting off the sun as shards fell to the ground in a rain of diamonds. The Dullahan glanced at Dagda, whose expression closely matched something of horror and rage. The Dullahan looked to some of the creatures who didn't seem bothered by their broken barrier. Thundering footsteps ran toward him; without looking, the Dullahan raised his palm toward the threat. He turned just as Dagda stopped nearly inches from his face. The god was stopped by the Dullahan's magic. Black tendrils of energy curled around the deity, rendering him fully paralyzed. The only thing he could do was watch the rest of the Dullahan's plan unfold.

The Dullahan pointed two fingers at the creatures before him and dragged the fingers through the air. As they slowly moved, so did the creatures. By this point, they started to cry for their master to help. And from the corner of the Dullahan's eyes, all he could see was the god turning red in the face. It made no difference to the Dullahan; they could easily be recreated. It was highly illogical to him to form such a bond over beasts without power or usefulness. The Dullahan turned his attention again to his magic and guided the beasts toward the sky, where, with his mind, he formed a portal to another world. A skill that his masters instilled in him, which seemed like a millennium ago. The Dullahan released his magical grasp and watched the creatures fly helplessly into the unknown. The portal closed as the last creature entered, leaving the other creatures running around in fear—their peace utterly destroyed.

The binds that held Dagda unwound, disappearing in a wisp of smoke. The god fell to his knees helplessly, appearing just as broken as his world. A massive hand went to his face as large tears fell, splashing to the ground and making a puddle within seconds.

"What...what have you done?" he said between sobs.

"I did you a favor. I proved that there was a flaw in your creation."

"By destroying it?" Dagda now stared up at the Dullahan, his eyes red and face blotchy.

"Would you have believed me otherwise?"

"Just...just leave me alone. I do not wish to see you again," Dagda replied, waving him off.

"So be it, I had no intentions of staying. Besides, this was merely a test," the Dullahan replied, taking a last look around.

Dagda stared at the monstrous being, his mouth gaping open, "Test, you were performing a...test!"

Hearing the anger rise in his voice, the Dullahan simply nodded and began walking away, "Yes, and we passed."

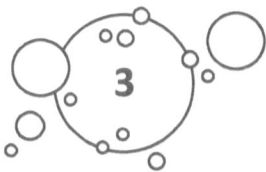

3

Danu stood beside a crying Dagda, pleading with his creator. She raised her arms, gesturing to the unusual creatures Dagda created—obviously inquiring about how and why many were missing. At least, that's how it appeared to the Dullahan as he stood back on his desolate planet, watching the chaos in Dagda's world unfold. He stared into a black mist that acted as a screen that displayed the dramatic scene. With one finger, he touched the mist, turning up the volume.

"It was not me; I swear it! Why would I ever do such a thing?"

Danu stared at Dagda, hands on her hips, "I do not know. Perhaps you were unhappy with the gifts I gave you?"

"That is false. I love my world—my creatures. It was the foreign celestial being. I cannot remember his name. He did not speak of himself. You must believe me. I speak only the truth."

A flicker of fear crossed Danu's face before a smile grew, "Oh, my dear child, I am afraid that you are mistaken. There is no creature here other than the ones you already know of—your celestial sisters and brothers."

How patronizing. This is to be expected coming from Danu. My influence on that tiny world seems to have unsettled her enough to where she is blaming her creations for mistakes that are not their own. She is reacting exactly how we expected. We must proceed with the rest of our plan.

The Dullahan slid his hand through the mist before him and watched as the scene disappeared. It quickly reformed into another scene—the entire solar system. His black eyes darted from one planet to another, calculating his next move. The planets closest to Danu would be an unnecessary risk and may cause a delay in the plan. But, the planets near his typically went unnoticed, at least from what he had seen. In fact, she had never visited the darker planets in the years he had known Danu. He only observed them on occasion whenever their tempers flared up. The Dullahan preferred to understand what triggered his opponents. It was a better way of controlling them should the time arise. And that time was now. His first option was the god, Arwn. This particular deity delighted himself in death. Like his dark celestial siblings, Arwn's planet was primarily barren. Still, with one exception—it was a planet full of graves. Whether they were empty or not, the Dullahan didn't know. He never viewed the planet long enough to find out. It was relatively insignificant to the overall plan. Besides, the god rarely dwelt on his planet as he was often found on the next planet. The goddess who ruled that planet thrived off lust, which Arwn gladly provided for her. Although the two would make a good duo for the Dullahan's plan, he knew their minds would not be on the task he had for them.

The Dullahan nearly ran out of ideas until he came upon another planet orbiting off in the distance. Its blood-red surface radiated a dark energy that seemed to beckon the Dullahan. And he eagerly heeded its call. His feet landed on the planet with a splash, and thick red liquid spattered his legs. His eyebrows were raised with intrigue. He glanced around the red planet to find that streams of liquid flowed all around, with few areas of solid ground to stand. The dry spots of the land were black and porous. Even the atmosphere had a red haze. The Dullahan's eyes narrowed as he sniffed the air. Iron was the closest element he could associate with the smell. He stared at his bare feet and watched the red pool cover his pale, alien skin. He dipped his hand in the liquid and rubbed his long fingers together. He stretched out his tongue as the tip flicked his fingers. Blood. He immediately identified that as a mixture of humans and animals. The specifics were a bit shaky but also irrelevant. He found his perfect planet. Finding the deity was going to be a different story. There was no sign of a dwelling or a hint of life. From his feet to the horizon, the Dullahan could only see various types of weaponry scattered haphazardly about. He would have thought he stumbled upon a battleground if there had been corpses. He opened his mouth to call out to the deity, hoping his greeting would reach their ears. But not even a sound escaped his alien lips as the ground started to shake.

Blood started bubbling all around him, and the atmosphere grew warmer. Were any typical deity standing in the blood, the Dullahan imagined they may not survive the boiling liquid. This, at the very least, would provide him the privacy he needed for the next phase of the plan. With the bubbling reaching its peak, the ground began to quake as geysers of blood shot toward the black sky. Blood rained upon the Dullahan as he watched with intrigue as the geysers flowed into a physical form. At first, it looked to be a rather long flowing skirt, but the blood was alive in its own way, and from the waist, a darker red bodice was formed, followed by cherry red arms, a neck, and a bald head. The creature opened its black eyes and mouth, revealing no teeth—just darkness.

"It is not often that I receive visitors. Who are you, and what do you want?" asked the creature, its voice as hollow as a cavern.

"I seek the ruler of this unique planet."

"Why?

Despite having almost no facial expression, the Dullahan could hear the tint of suspicion in the creature's voice. He glanced around again at the war zone around him and then looked back at the deity. Its very presence radiated power, power that he only felt during times of intense war. This goddess wouldn't listen to reason or even false charisma as Dagda did. No, she would only comprehend battle strategy.

"I have a proposition for them."

The deity tilted her head ever so slightly, indicating she was intrigued by his words, "They call me Macha. Why should I want anything from you?"

"I can make you the most powerful creature this universe has ever seen—unlimited power that would make even your darker neighbors tremble."

A strangled gurgle emitted from Macha's mouth, which sounded eerily like a laugh. Her body started flowing around him, pacing the land before her, "And what is in it for you?" She was clever. The Dullahan had to give her that much credit. Macha would not be so easily fooled. He had to give her information she wanted to hear and believe. He feigned a smirk and opened his arms in a defensive gesture.

"All I ask is that you defeat my enemies for me."

"Immeasurable power is what you offer; all you ask in return is to defeat your enemies. Surely, if you can offer me this, you should be able to do it yourself."

"And rob you of this grand opportunity? You are the Goddess of War, are you not? This is your field of expertise."

Stroking her ego seemed to work for the Dullahan. Macha's pacing slowed. She stopped and stared into the distance before facing the Dullahan, "Tell me, what enemies should a creature like you have?"

"They are not in this solar system, at least not yet."

She gurgled a laugh once more and crossed her arms, "You see the future now, do you?"

The Dullahan cast his gaze on the ground, letting the flowing blood momentarily make him lose focus. He thought about how far he had come with the plan. Macha would make the perfect subject for the next phase, even better than he initially anticipated. He looked up at the goddess, "You are mistaken. I *am* the future."

***

His last comment seemed to work as Macha immediately jumped on board with his elusive plan. At first, he found her blind faith to be a concern, but eventually, he found a way to use it to his advantage. Like his test with Dagda, the Dullahan began infecting Macha's planet with magic. But it was a slow process and slightly different. Instead of just his magic, he started taking some of the elements of his own planets and attaching them to areas of Macha's planet where it would take root and grow like a cancer. Over time, he saw her growing more attached to him and even listening to everything he suggested. To appease her thirst for war, he'd sometimes create blood creatures to have her fight. Little did she know that she was mostly fighting herself. But she seemed perfectly content and joyful even to do this. All the while, he assured her that this was training for the real battle.

And everything had been going well for several decades at least. Macha was blissfully unaware of how much power she lost during this time. Until an anomaly interfered with the plan. The other two darker planet deities arrived on Macha's planet unexpectedly. Arwn sauntered toward her, casually looking about the land. Although he tried to hide it, his expression revealed that he was silently judging Macha's taste in decor, or maybe lack thereof. Trailing behind him, as if making a grand entrance, was the Goddess of Lust herself, Morrighan. The creature barely wore a thing except for a dark silk fabric that loosely fell across her dress and barely covered her waist. It appeared she had to leave her home abruptly and threw on the closest material she could find. Not that appearances mattered to the Dullahan; he did not desire such things.

Arwn settled on a spot near the protruding remains of a torture device. He began examining it as if he were interested. Still, from what the Dullahan knew of him, Arwn was only along for the journey. He didn't much care about anything that didn't have to do with his mistress. The Dullahan watched his subject as her expression rapidly went from annoyance to disgust. Morrighan's seductive stride seemed to set Macha off in a bitter way. The Dullahan detected some animosity between the goddesses, possibly an ancient feud long before his arrival. Whatever the reason, Macha seemed to be handling it well. Perhaps whatever Morrighan had to say would work in his favor.

"You seem to be a bit lost, Morrighan. Did you misplace your planet?" asked Macha, her tone laced with acid.
"On the contrary, my dear Macha. I noticed that the aura around your planet has changed, but now I can see why," Morrighan said in her sultry tone. Her dark eyes fixed on the Dullahan at the last bit. She stared at his alien form and smiled, "Tell me what is the name of your creature?"

Macha looked from Morrighan to the Dullahan. He could tell Macha felt inferior around this specific deity. Before she could speak, the Dullahan replied, "I do not have a name, though some have given me the title of the Dullahan. And...I can speak for myself."

"Oh, can you now?" Morrighan's gaze went to a deathly glare as she shifted her attention back to Macha, "You gave your creation a mind of its own, it seems."

Feeling threatened, Macha growled, "What are you doing here, Morrighan?"

"I'm just looking for some fun. I wondered if you and the Dullahan would care to visit my world for...a party."

"We are not interested in anything you have to offer. Feel free to leave at any time," the Dullahan spoke up simply.

He was testing the waters now. Morrighan would not be challenged, and he found it surprising that Arwn had now focused his attention on the conversation. Quietly, the God of Death inched toward the group and stared at the Dullahan. He stepped close to him and took in a whiff of his scent like a dog. His eyes narrowed, "He is not of this solar system."

"What gave it away, my Pet?" asked Morrighan sarcastically.

"No, he does not smell of life or death. He is not even alive in the sense that we are."

"Why should the question of my existence matter? Macha and I are content being alone. Now, perhaps it would be best that you leave now."

The Dullahan looked at Macha, whose expression hadn't wavered. She still glared at Morrighan threateningly, not even concerned that the Dullahan had been speaking for her nearly this entire time. He looked from Arwn to Morrighan, who exchanged looks of confusion and concern. From what he knew of this dark trio, this type of hostility never occurred. Macha always spoke for herself and rarely fought with Morrighan.

Morrighan wasn't going to settle for that answer. Instead, she tried a different tactic, one she clearly thought would work. Morrighan slowly walked toward the Dullahan, allowing her already risqué outfit to drop only a few inches, revealing more of her body than necessary. The Dullahan's gaze shifted from her to Arwn, whose mouth curved into a smirk. He looked back to Morrighan, whose every move was over-accentuated, and a sickly-sweet aroma wafted toward him. With his alien eyes, he focused them on the energy field surrounding the goddess. Bright pink tendrils emanated from her body, wrapping around him. This unusual ability must be what humans would compare to that of an aphrodisiac. Within moments, she was next to him, her bare shoulder barely touching his bare flesh. Her scent grew stronger as she leaned closer to him and whispered, "I will have you one day. Besides, I'm more fun!"

She lifted her head and stared at him. He glanced at her sideways and whispered back firmly, "Doubtful."

Had he cared about winning this pointless conversation, the Dullahan imagined that he'd find some semblance of joy in the expression of disgust plastered on Morrighan's face. In fact, Arwn shared a similar expression, though he appeared more afraid than anything. On the other hand, Macha seemed unfazed by the entire situation, almost as if she were lost in thought.

Arwn blindly reached for Morrighan, who backed away slowly. The second his hand touched her arm, the two vanished in a puff of smoke—their expressions of horror the last the Dullahan saw.

Satisfied with how that conversation ended, the Dullahan turned toward Macha, who was snapping out of her daydream. She looked at him, and the faint lines of her mouth turned up in a smile. He nodded, but not reassuring her, more because she had passed the test. Macha was entirely under his command, and she could do nothing about it. She was ready for the final stage of the plan, provided that she would survive.

The Dullahan sighed and said, "Now, where were we?"

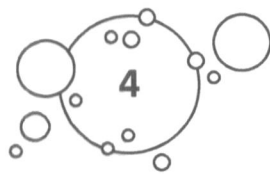

4

Macha didn't survive. However, the results of the final test did. But that was hundreds of years ago. The only remnants of the former goddess were the constant shrill screams in the Dullahan's memory. Not that it mattered. To him, those sounds were just the universe putting itself right, or rather, beginning to. With Macha out of his way, the Dullahan's real work could begin. And so it did. With her unwilling assistance, four new creatures were formed. Almost straightway, they began to work on the Dullahan's master plan, but it wasn't without its challenges. The first challenge being the creatures themselves. He never bothered to give them names as they were expendable creatures only meant for one purpose, much like Macha. But they, for some reason, found names to be necessary. Taghd, Siochain, Coimhlint, and Saol. Their names were of the same language as the other planets. Still, the Dullahan gathered that the language of the planets was ingrained in their DNA. He rarely called them by that name; he seldom tried to communicate with them directly at all. Most of the time, they were off on their own, conducting their own research around the solar system. Lately, the Dullahan found their efforts fruitless, and the brothers grew restless. Although he understood, they were after the same thing he was—death and blood. The monotony of the trials was soon to end as the Dullahan conjured a plan that would prove difficult but possible.

The Dullahan stood on his planet, staring out over the solar system. His gaze shifted from planet to planet, and he decided which was to be his next move. From the corner of his eyes, three lines of space dust floated from Macha's planet toward his in synchronism. They landed next to each other, the space dust piling into physical forms. When fully constructed, the four beings reminded the Dullahan very much of how the other planets portrayed themselves—humanoid. But they were still dark creatures, and that darkness dramatically reflected their appearance. Although they looked human, their flesh reflected the particles of space dust. And their black, demonic-like eyes could draw nearly anyone in like the power of a black hole. Their bodies were clothed in mainly black, but their style varied.

Taghd, whose main personality represented wrath, wore tight-fitting pants and a long-sleeve shirt. A high-collared cloak draped over his shoulders—the long material flowed with his every movement. His black hair spiked at the top. Crude piercings lined his right ear, and a scowl marred his face. His gaze attempted to bore into the Dullahan, but he was unfazed.

"Have you anything else for us? It has been far too long, and we have grown bored," Taghd said in a smooth, deep voice.

"Possibly," the Dullahan replied, looking back at the other planets.

"Possibly? You can give us more than that. What are you planning?" asked Saol.

The Dullahan looked at Saol. Unlike Taghd, this creature reveled in the concept of death. His wardrobe was less ostentatious as Taghd, but not by much. He wore a thick black vest with sharp spikes sticking up from his shoulders. The vest had very little design except for the stitching, which had no particular pattern. The vest wasn't bare, though. Attached to the shoulder spikes was a sheer black material that clung loosely to his arms and ended at his wrists. His pants were of a similar billowing style but as solid a color as his vest. The Dullahan looked back to the planets, his eyes focusing on one in particular, which belonged to the goddess Cerridwen. Her world was unlike the others in that there were humanoid creatures that called themselves Avalonians. They resembled much of the humans of Earth, but their biological makeup was mildly different. These creatures could detect planetary magic.

"You are having us go there. Why?" Siochian's gentler voice broke through his reverie.

The Dullahan's attention shot to the creature, who was very sharp and fed off negative emotions. But his primary personality was that of hatred. Siochain's black eyes were still staring at the planet, waiting for the Dullahan to give an answer. He wore less clothing than any of the others. In fact, the only things on his body were black pants and leather wristbands that concealed small blades—items he rarely used.

"I need the creatures that reside on that planet—the Avalonians."

"There is nothing remarkable about them. We have watched them since their creation," Coimhlint spoke up. His bare arms crossed across his chest in defiance. This particular creature lived for war, just like Macha. Like Saol, Coimhlint wore a vest, though the stitching sparkled more. Two massive swords crossed on his back, waiting for their master to wield them.

"On the contrary, they are a valuable asset to my plan. Observe," said the Dullahan, gesturing toward the planet Avalon. People, young and old, went about the land farming, fishing, and tending to animals. Some, who were better dressed, meandered around a large stone structure that housed the more elite rulers of the humans, "They are the perfect specimen."

"They are mere mortals. How can they be of any use to us?" asked Saol.

"Experimentation is their sole purpose," the Dullahan replied simply.

A bright shimmer caught the Dullahan's attention. A figure emerged from seemingly out of nowhere and floated on a cloud above the land. Cerridwen watched over her creations—human and fairy alike. Like any good deity, she watched over each one, staying as far out of their business as possible while ensuring they were well. Taghd cleared his throat, "That will pose a problem in your plan."

The Dullahan remained silent, continuously watching the beings on the land. His focus shifted to the ground as children played in the dirt. A little girl inhaled a cloud of dirt that a little boy kicked up. Her face contorted, and she let out a sneeze. He raised an eyebrow in curiosity and replied, "On the contrary. This will do just fine."

This new direction began almost immediately. The Dullahan realized it would prove difficult should Cerridwen uncover his plan, but he was patient, he had to be. With Coimhlint's unique power of disease, the Dullahan decided the best way to collect his specimens was to inflict slight illnesses on them. He'd allow his creations to pick the humans at random. Young, old, male, female—he didn't care. The more variables, the better he would understand how his tests would affect Earth humans. The process of procuring these humans was left entirely up to Dullahan's creatures. It wasn't that he wasn't curious; he just didn't care, just so long as they kept under the radar from Cerridwen and, more importantly, Danu.

The Dullahan did sit in on the testing of these subjects. He would allow his creations to start the initial process, testing the humans to see their endurance level. When he was satisfied with one human, he'd take them to the final stages, infusing the subject with minerals from his planet—elements that would ultimately alter the person's biological makeup. No one survived. Trial after trial, the Dullahan went through countless Avalonians for hundreds of years. Each one proved the same. He was missing a key component. Even the creations seemed to get a bit antsy with no results. He eventually suggested they take their experimentations to the next level, but the creations violently protested his suggestions, resulting in a needless fight between them and the Dullahan. Their fight was quickly interrupted when Danu paid them a visit.

But it wasn't just the Dullahan she had come to see, it was his creations. However, they were more confused than the Dullahan as they had never seen Danu before. The Dullahan stared at Danu blankly, waiting for her to make another move.

Her gaze fell upon the four creations, and her expression seemed firm and cold, but when her attention turned to the Dullahan, her eyes narrowed, and the corners of her lips turned down. Her voice was just as dark, "I will get straight to the point. What have you been planning?"

"I have been following the same plan since we arrived at this solar system. Why confront me now?"

Danu pursed her lips, "You are disrupting the natural order of things."

"Correction. *Your* order, you mean."

Danu tilted her head toward the four creatures and said, "What are they, and why send them to Avalon?"

"Both are experiments," the Dullahan replied without looking at the creatures. Already, he could feel their confused stares directed toward him.

"To what end?"

"That is not relevant to you."

"It is if you are stealing human Avalonians. Cerridwen is becoming suspicious, and I cannot conceal your identity for long."

The Dullahan shook his head, "Why does the knowledge of my existence threaten you so much? Are you afraid that I will reveal the truth behind who you are?"

Again, she ignored his question, "Let us make a compromise. I will allow you to proceed with this *plan*. As long as you hand your illicit creation over to me."

"How are they illicit?"

"I saw what happened to Macha," she replied almost angrily.

The Dullahan cast a glance at the creatures, who exchanged nervous looks. *They know something, but how?* He thought. His attention returned to Danu, "Yet you did nothing to prevent it. Clearly, your compassion is selective."

An awkward silence filled the air as Danu stared at the Dullahan, clearly fuming. The Dullahan looked at his creation and watched them exchange looks. Based on their varying changes in expressions, he would have thought they were speaking telepathically. But he knew better. They had powers, but not that kind.

On the other hand, he didn't know these creatures besides what he created them for. He looked at them and judging by their body language, it was apparent they were planning something, and perhaps it could alter his plans. Perhaps Danu's suggestion wasn't a bad idea after all.

The Dullahan broke the silence, "I will agree to your terms. I have no more use for them."

The fierce gazes from the creations were enough to burn a hole in a man. Fortunately for the Dullahan, he wasn't a man and didn't care. He didn't lie to Danu; it was the truth. At the moment, he had no use for them, and that's all he created them for—to be tools in his master plan. With the creations muttering amongst themselves, a triumphant smirk grew on Danu's face.

"Then it is settled," she spoke, her tone equally victorious. Danu turned to the creations, her voice silencing their mutterings, "You four will remain on your planet for the duration of your existence."

The four erupted with complaints. But Danu held up her hand, and somehow, that gesture immediately silenced them. "You will all have a section of your planet that will be your domain. And you may never leave it."

"You mean to separate us from each other? For what purpose exactly?" asked Taghd. The Dullahan detected curiosity in his voice rather than fear, which he found odd for the creature with the most wrath.

"I would prefer to keep a close eye on you. Besides, perhaps this time of solitude will give you all some time to think for yourself. Who knows, you may find that you like your new dwelling."

"I think you mean prison," said Siochain bitterly.

"You will not know any different. The moment you arrive on your planet, your memories will be stripped, and you will be given new ones," Danu explained. Given her detailed instructions, the Dullahan guessed she was making this up as she went along based on the creations' disgusted expressions.

Although one seemed less appalled than the others— Taghd. He looked concerned but was more preoccupied with how the others were reacting. But there was more to it than that. The Dullahan glanced at Taghd, searching for any reason why he'd be the calmest of them all. It was there, at the corner of his eye, that the Dullahan caught a slight movement. It was so insignificant that the Dullahan almost missed it. Taghd had his arms crossed defiantly, mimicking the attitude of the others. Still, the fingers closest to his body wiggled, and tiny sparks bounced between his tips. Danu didn't seem to take notice of the spell he was casting, and oddly enough, neither did the Dullahan. For a brief moment, while Danu gloated a bit more and proceeded to relay new information about their prison world, the Dullahan and Taghd locked gazes. At first, Taghd's face was expressionless, and that's when the Dullahan found out. His creation had a plan of some kind, almost as if they knew something like this would occur. The Dullahan shook these thoughts from his mind as they were irrelevant. As long as Danu didn't kill his creations, he could still use them for his plans for the future.

Ignoring their silent protests, Danu raised her hands, and gold sparkled from her fingertips. The Dullahan's creations disappeared in a cloud of golden smoke. With the smoke floating in place, Danu took her index finger and casually directed the creations to their new planet. The Dullahan watched as they landed on their planet in a flash.

"There, that is done," said Danu matter-of-factly, "I meant what I said, Dullahan. You may proceed with whatever you are planning."

"I was unaware I required your permission," he replied casually.

The goddess turned her full attention to her enemy, and a scowl crossed her face, "You are in my solar system now, Dullahan. You will always require my permission."

"Assuming something more powerful is not already in control."

"What could be more powerful than me? These other planets? You even? I do not think you realize that there is more power in influence and charisma than actual magic."

The Dullahan nodded, absorbing her words and choosing his next carefully, "Perhaps, but your *talents* can only take you as far as your lies. They will eventually realize who and what you really are. At that point, all the attention will be on you, just as you always wanted."

Danu's scowl turned into rage. She walked toward him— every step accentuating her authority. She stopped barely centimeters from the Dullahan's face, who showed no emotion, "And what will become of you, Great Seer?"

"I have not lied; therefore, I will be invisible until I want to be seen," he replied. "I am no seer as you say. I am simply stating the inevitable."

"We shall see," Danu hissed. The goddess turned on her heel, satisfied with having the final word. But, the Dullahan expected this reaction from her, just as he expected her to attempt to foil his current plan. As usual, he was always two steps ahead of her.

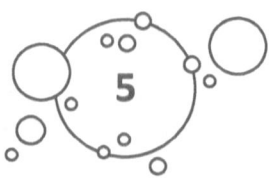

5

Avalon. The planet never held much interest for the Dullahan. It was always a bustling little world inhabited initially by fairies and dragons who co-existed peacefully until the two rulers of both species had an argument that led to a battle. This magical battle resulted in a unique creation—humans. But not like the humans of Earth. No, these humans all contained magic in their genetic code. All could sense magic to some degree or another, but others could do magic. These were known among the Avalonians as the Chosen. Their magic was considered a gift by the fairies and dragons. However, none of the humans knew their origin story except by legend. These Chosen became the rulers of the human domain. For centuries, humans lived in peace. This was mainly due to Avalon's goddess, Cerridwen. She was appalled by the behavior of her original creations, and she split their lands.

The dragons felt uncertain about these *accidents* and were content living by themselves. The fairies were more curious, especially one in particular who often found secret ways of entering the human domain. But this wasn't an ordinary fairy; this was the queen—Nimue.

She used her magic to make herself appear more like them, but the Avalonians weren't the wiser, except for one—King Arthur. He had no reason to give her secret away, though, for he fell in love with her. Or, so she thought. At this time, the Dullahan was still working on his creations, so he didn't pay much attention to their little love story. But it would soon turn to tragedy and pave the way for a cataclysm of planetary events.

Her human lover soon found another, one more of his species. This enraged the fairy queen, and she soon wreaked havoc on the human domain. This was the Dullahan's perfect opportunity to swing in and introduce himself. Nimue was weak, and everything can change in a moment of emotional weakness.

***

Nimue stood on the edge of her floating land, staring down at the land that once belonged to her. The castle was abuzz with an evening celebration—a wedding celebration. King Arthur married his lover, Guinevere, and everyone appeared happy. They had seemingly forgotten about the mysterious beauty Arthur once loved. Most of the Avalonians turned their admiration and even worship towards the dragons, leaving Nimue and her fairies feared and, at times, disregarded. The Dullahan discreetly appeared behind her, leaning casually against the wall of her castle. He watched her every movement, deciding how to initiate the conversation.

"Celebrating as if I never even mattered," Nimue whispered to herself.

"Of course you did not," he said a little too casually.

The fairy queen whipped around, her long, red hair slashing at the wind. Her eyes narrowed at him, trying to focus on his shadowy figure, "Who goes there? How did you get past my guards?"

The Dullahan emerged from the shadows, "Like you, I have my own special powers."

As the creature stepped into the moonlight, Nimue's jaw dropped, and she stepped back in fear, "What...what happened to your head?"

"But an old battle scar," he replied with a sly grin.

"Battle? I have never heard of a battle occurring."

"It was long before your time."

There. A faint smile flickered on Nimue's face. The Dullahan successfully grabbed her attention. She partially turned back to the human domain as she crossed her arms, "While I appreciate you validating what I already know, you do not know anything about me or my life."

The Dullahan had now come to the queen's side, "On the contrary, I have watched you since the goddess herself formed you."

Nimue looked down at the disembodied head and gave him a suspicious look, "Why show so much interest in me?"

The Dullahan continued pushing his charm, "Because you are special, something that little king could not see."

"Well, he is not the only one. All of the humans once adored me and my fairies. Now, we are the enemy, and I am not certain where I went wrong."

"They fear your power. Most primitive species react this way."

Nimue sighed and lowered her head, "If you have been watching me as you say, then you know that is not fully true."

The Dullahan lifted the hand, holding his head until it was near eye level with Nimue. This small action did precisely as he had expected. Her rage was lessening and turning into sorrow. And when someone is sorrowful, they tend to express more than they think, "Everything was going well until the child came...Arthur's and mine."

Two different species procreating? That was not an anticipated result, the Dullahan thought. This information gave him more to think about. He looked down on the human domain and adjusted his eyesight to see the small human figures. The king and his new queen stood on a balcony of the castle overlooking their people. In between them stood a young boy of about five years. He smiled, but the Dullahan could sense a strong emotion behind that—confusion. Based on his study of the human race, this child was probably wondering what became of his biological mother. Due to the fact King Arthur and Nimue did not separate amicably, the king probably told his son a false tale. But that's what fascinated the Dullahan about human children. They never seemed to fully believe everything they were told. Their imaginations were powerful, whether Earth children or the magical Avalonians. These imaginations helped them form the thoughts that would lead them into adulthood.

"I must have missed that. How did the child remain with his father?"

Nimue scoffed, "If you ask why I did not fight to keep him, you are wrong. I fought hard and pleaded with the king relentlessly. But his horrid advisers believed I just wanted power. Truthfully, I believe they were afraid of what we created. It had never been done before. I suppose I should be relieved that they did not just have him killed."

"What is stopping you this very moment? The child is down there on that balcony, and I know you have ways of sneaking into the human domain. Those Avalonians should not matter. They are powerless against you."

"He would be hurt in the crossfires, and I could not let that happen. Besides, they used dragon magic on him. Fairy magic and dragon magic do not mix. We are the opposing forces of this world. I could not rescue my son even if I wanted to."

A single tear fell down her cheek at the last word. The Dullahan redirected the angle of his conversation to tug more at her heartstrings, "Perhaps when he is older, he will decide for himself what he wants."

"Unlikely, they will continue using dragon magic on him so long as they think I cannot see him."

"They have yet to meet my magic," the Dullahan said slyly.

"Why would you help me? You have nothing to gain," she replied.

"On the contrary, I have everything to gain. Many years ago, I lost a companion, someone who helped me on my journey to uncover the secrets of humanity. If you help me, I will make you so powerful that even those dragons cannot stop you."

"Humanity? What do you care about that?"

"I do not, but my masters do. Humans hold the secret to their existence."

"And you do not question them?"

Nimue was not like Macha. There was intelligence behind her raw emotions—intelligence that asked dangerous questions. He had to take more control over the conversation and future ones for this to work.

"I have no need. I was created to gather intelligence, which is what I am doing. Will you assist me?"

"For my son, Lancelot?" Nimue looked back at the Dullahan and, with a sliver of coldness in her eyes, said, "Anything."

For weeks after their introduction, the Dullahan and Nimue practiced magic together. At first, the Dullahan stayed with Nimue in her castle, observing every aspect of her power. Each time she used her magic for a large spell, the Dullahan discreetly analyzed her movements and the method to her end results. Nimue paid him no mind; she thought he was watching her with fascination or, at the very least, intrigue, which only fueled her talents. When the Dullahan wasn't with her, he was back on his own planet, trying to replicate her spells with his power, but each test ended with less than adequate results. It took him several different experiments for each replicated spell, but he had the patience for it. This was a virtue that he soon found Nimue did not possess.

Each day, he watched Nimue look out from her tower and on Camelot. Tears flowed from her eyes when Lancelot played in the castle gardens. But those tears quickly turned from sorrow to rage when the king and queen appeared. Showing off her magic soon became a thing of the past as her sole focus was back on revenge. The Dullahan rapidly changed tactics and asked her to show him what her spells could do to the humans. With her mind set on vengeance, she suggested taking someone from inside the castle. The Dullahan liked her gumption, but taking someone who'd be noticeably missed was not in their best interest at this stage of the game. He suggested one of the farmers or one of the poorer families to start with. Although she agreed with a change of pace, Nimue grew bored of playing with her human victims. Altering their appearances and, at times, morphing them into partial animals didn't seem enough for her; she wanted more. That is when the Dullahan suggested she try to transport them to different areas of the planet. She found it quite humorous when she saw their confused and often frightened faces upon landing in the dragon's domain.

"I do believe that is the most frightened expression I have ever seen!" exclaimed Nimue, turning away from her floating mirror. In the image stood a young woman with two grotesque horns protruding from her head and eyes like a goat. She stood among small dragons who looked at her with great curiosity.

"I do not know about that. The beasts seem more afraid of her," replied the Dullahan, leaning against the wall of her chambers.

Nimue skipped up to him like an infatuated schoolgirl. The fairy queen had grown close to her teacher, and the Dullahan humored her. She looped her arm through his and leaned down to give him a kiss on his head. He forced a smile. It felt as unnatural to him as the young woman felt with horns. He allowed these moments of false passion for the simple fact that Nimue needed it. She was alone in this large world and even in her solar system. Even her creator seemed divorced from the matters of her creation, particularly the fairies. But the Dullahan assumed that Danu might have had a hand in that. Either way, he never let Nimue's emotional needs distract him from his ultimate goal. In fact, today was the perfect day to introduce the next step in his plan. The Dullahan gently pulled away from his student and walked toward a nearby table where a goblet of fairy water and fruit sat. He took the goblet and dumped out its aqua-colored contents. He glanced at his student and pulled out a vile of dark blue liquid. She gave him a quizzical look, and the edge of her lips turned up.

"What is that?" she asked, slowly coming forward.

The Dullahan poured the liquid into the goblet and offered it to her, "This liquid will allow you to access my...power."

Cautiously, she took the offer from his grasp and lifted the lip of the goblet to her nose. Her nose scrunched up as she deeply inhaled the scent, and her eyes squeezed shut, "That smells dreadful. Should I at least know what I am drinking?"

The Dullahan paused and carefully chose his next words. He put the vile back in a concealed compartment in his vest pocket, "You might call it a potion—one from my home world."

She put the cup to her lips and paused, looking at the Dullahan. "You never talk about your world. Why is that?"

"You are diverting. Drink the potion. It will help you," he said, feigning a smile.

Nimue shrugged and smiled before tilting the cup back and drinking the liquid in one gulp. Her reaction to the taste was almost identical to when she first smelled it, though it was accompanied by retching this time. But nothing protruded from her mouth; it was as if her body had immediately absorbed the foreign potion. Nimue stumbled backward, dropping the goblet to the ground. She leaned against the closest wall for support as her body violently shook from the effects. Her breathing became shallow, and as she slid to the ground, her eyes slowly closed. Silence clung in the air as she exhaled her last breath. The Dullahan stared at her cold figure, then glanced around the room to be sure suspicious fairies weren't lurking. When he looked back on Nimue, her eyes suddenly opened, and she gasped for air. Her hand went to her throat, pulling at the proverbial rope around her neck.

"Help me?" she choked, her voice rough, "That potion nearly killed me."

"Oh, but it did kill you. That was the intent," the Dullahan said matter-of-factly.

Nimue looked at her master, horrified, "I don't understand."

Footsteps echoed outside her chambers, and in came an elf guard. He looked at the Dullahan with suspicion—his eyes narrowed. Then, he turned his attention to the fairy queen, "My Lady, is everything all right?"

The Dullahan raised an eyebrow at the elf and then answered for her, "Your timing is most opportune. Your queen was just about to practice her newfound magic."

"I was? I mean, yes, I was," she replied, catching the Dullahan's glance.

"Go on, Nimue, attempt to pause time," the Dullahan replied, his eyes back on the loyal guard.

The elf looked from his mistress to her companion. A shiny flicker of light caught his attention and he glanced down at an empty goblet laying forgotten on the ground—its dark contents splattered all over the floor.

The elf returned her attention to Nimue concealing his concern as best he could, "With all due respect, My Queen, that does not seem—"

Suddenly, the elf guard stood frozen, his worried gaze frozen on Nimue, and his mouth hung open mid-sentence. The Dullahan looked at Nimue, who appeared less frightened than he had anticipated. No, she was filled with awe and excitement.

"I did that?" she asked in astonishment.

The Dullahan watched as she approached her guard and waved her hand before his face. Realizing he was frozen, she rushed to the window and looked down on her kingdom. The Dullahan walked up to her side and gazed out over the land, watching as other fairies walked and occasionally flew around like nothing ever happened.

"How...how is that possible?" Nimue asked, looking back at the frozen guard.

"You desired to pause time, so it paused. With my power combined with yours, all you need to do to cast spells is think them."

"So why was only my guard frozen?"

"You need to be specific with your thoughts. In time, you will be able to pause time anywhere and everywhere. Now, unfreeze him."

Nimue looked at the guard, whose mouth almost immediately began to move, "—wise. How did you get to the window so quickly? Were you not just by the wall?"

The fairy queen looked at the Dullahan in confusion; he seemed to already know her question, "Time moves differently for those who have been frozen in time. As far as your guard is concerned, no time has passed. The longer the time is frozen, the more effect it will have. Do not worry; you will grow in this new power quickly."

Nimue smiled at her teacher as she descended the stairs, "Come, I believe our lessons start now!"

As the Dullahan followed Nimue, he brushed past the guard, who refused to take his eyes off the foreigner. Suddenly, a cold hand grabbed the Dullahan's arm. The Dullahan stopped and casually turned his head toward the guard. He looked up at him as the elf revealed his hand covered in the same liquid Nimue had drunk.

The elf looked from his soaked hand to the Dullahan, waiting for an answer, "You are bleeding."

The Dullahan moved his head to glance at his arm. A faint trickle of blood streamed down his arm from a poorly bandaged wound. Believing the elf's initial grab had something to do with his wound reopening, the Dullahan stared at him straight-faced, "It appears so."

With his tight grip around her magic, the Dullahan watched as Nimue tried to figure out her new powers. She continued to be blissfully unaware of how she got it, but the Dullahan preferred it that way. He expected the elf guard who had interrupted them to be too afraid to tell his mistress that what she really drank was the Dullahan's blood.

But, given her unquestioned loyalty and devotion to him, the Dullahan doubted she would have been phased. However, she didn't dive as quickly into her new gift as he had expected. He often found her watching the castle for her son. During these moments, she seemed to forget she had the power to just snatch him away from Camelot and take him to another world where they could start their life over. It made no sense to the Dullahan. When he carefully prodded her to move forward with her plans to rescue the child, she simply gave him a sad look. Each time he asked, Nimue would reply that it'd only place the child in harm's way. There was no way to persuade her. During these times, the Dullahan often contemplated the situation on his planet. At times, he wondered if Nimue was the correct candidate for his test or if perhaps someone else should take the position. He had no genuine time restraints—he was there until his experiment was complete.

"Nimue had qualities that Macha possessed. I was certain she would make an acceptable replacement," the Dullahan said to the starry sky. He nodded to the voice in his head, as always, "I understand. We have all the time in the world to find someone more suitable. Perhaps—"

The Dullahan paused. A strange sensation shot through his alien form. He lifted his hands to his face, and his veins became more prominent. He stared at them in wonder as they became so visible he could almost see the blood rushing through them. His body surged with an energy he had yet to experience. He looked around him, wondering if the energy came from the planet. Still, as his eyes skimmed the horizon, a bright light flickered from Avalon. He quickly forgot his former conversation and brought his hands in front of him, creating a hologram in the atmosphere. He passed his hand over the screen until he found the scene that piqued his interest. For a moment, he stood frozen, uncertain of how to react. Then, he cocked his head to the side as if intrigued by what he was seeing.

Before him stood Nimue; a bright glow engulfed her body as tears of rage streaked down her flushed cheeks. On the far side of the screen, the Dullahan could see an old nursemaid and a child running away from her. He frowned in concentration. He didn't recognize either of them until he noticed a group of people to the side. He saw a young couple staring off after the child. The woman wept bitterly while the man consoled his wife. His attention turned to Nimue, and his soft, comforting expression turned to utter hatred. It was there, in his eyes, that he recognized the male human as Lancelot.

If this is Nimue's son, how long have I been away? When did he develop to this extent?

The Dullahan shook off this irrelevant thought and continued to watch the chaos that was about to unfold. Nimue extended her long arm out toward the fleeing figures and screamed. The glow around her grew so bright it nearly blinded the Dullahan. He quickly swiped the hologram away and looked down at Avalon. As his alien eyes adjusted to the darkness, that bright light shot straight up and slowly wrapped around the planet. The planet stood still for a moment until it started to crack in various places. The cracks grew so large that chunks of the land pulled apart from the planet and drifted off into space. The Dullahan stared at the remains of Avalon. He leaned forward, thoroughly intrigued by the site before him. Suddenly, a flash of another planet revealed itself between the cracks. It was a brief moment, but one his eyes could catch. It flashed twice more as the land masses of Avalon pulled themselves together as if nothing ever happened. But something did. He knew, from that moment, Avalon would never be the same.

The Dullahan waited a few Avalon days to see if anything else would happen to the world, but nothing did. It was as quiet as it was before Nimue's meltdown. That is, until *she* arrived on his planet. Danu sauntered toward him in her usual, overbearing manner.

"You have really caused quite a stir on Avalon, Dullahan."

The Dullahan refused to acknowledge her presence and stared at Avalon. Danu's steps came closer. She stopped by his side and continued prodding, "Is your silence denial?"

"You assume too much."

"What else am I supposed to do? No one else could have given the fairy that much power," said Danu defensively. Pausing in her emotional outburst, she gave him a suspicious look, "By the way, how *did* you manage to do that—cause that explosion?"

"That was not me. That was Nimue—well, not entirely, I suppose."

"Explain," she demanded, her voice growing fierce.

The Dullahan shrugged nonchalantly, "No need. My mission here has been fulfilled."

A dangerous silence grew between the two until Danu rolled her eyes and spat, "I do not believe that for a second. You always have a plan."

He nodded and finally looked at her with a curious expression, "That is where we have something in common."

A flash of horror crossed Danu's face. She flung her long dress around and stalked off in a fury, "If your mission is completed, then you will have no reason to stay. Do not delay."

The Dullahan watched as Danu disappeared. He turned back to the planets, focusing on Avalon again. He peered further onto the planet and watched Nimue pace her chambers, crying and throwing objects against the walls. With his hands, the Dullahan made a circular motion in the atmosphere, creating an orb. He let it free float as he spoke into it.

"Are you finished?"

Nimue stopped short of throwing a vase against a wall. She looked around her and, with a quaking, hoarse voice, said, "Who said that?"

"Who do you think?" asked the Dullahan, rather impatient.

A faded smile crossed her lips as she replied, "Master? But how is that possible? You cannot be here!"

"You are correct. I am not there but in your mind. Only you can hear me at this moment."

Nimue sat down on her massive bed, taking this information in. She wiped away a stray tear and said, "We have been caught. My creator has limited my abilities, and I can no longer access anything beyond my land. I—I don't even know what happened. I just became so furious."

"You did something no creature in your solar system could do. With our powers combined, you could open a permanent portal to another world far from yours."

"I heard murmurings about such a thing, but I didn't know it to be true," said Nimue, contemplating. "What was the point of it all? It did not give me the respect I desired."

"No, at least not right now."

Nimue rose from her bed and walked over to her balcony, which overlooked her land and the human domain. She placed her hands on the railing and said, "What do you mean?"

I have her attention; this should do nicely.

"Achieving what one desires takes much longer than you have attempted. If you follow my commands, you will get everything you want."

Nimue scoffed, "I tried that already. Look where that led me."

"I did not tell you to create a portal. That was all your own doing. You must rein in your emotions for this to succeed."

Nimue sighed, closed her eyes, and looked back at the human domain silently. The Dullahan waited patiently for her response.

She nodded as if agreeing to her inner voice, then replied, "I understand. What is our next move?"

"I am glad you asked," he said, content he subdued her tantrum.

The pair made a rather foolproof plan, or so they believed. The Dullahan decided to lay low for the time being, at least long enough to convince Danu he had no interest in continuing his plan with Nimue. Although Danu would always be suspicious, she left them alone. This gave the duo time to continue with their plan. Nimue created an orb similar to the Dullahan's at the bottom of her lake, a place few water fairies explored. With this orb and practice, she could communicate with the Dullahan and keep an eye on the humans that accidentally came to Earth.

This led Nimue to wonder what stories would be said of their journey to Earth. She brought these thoughts to the Dullahan, who brushed them off as nothing to be concerned with. He educated her on humanity. Humans, on all Earths, were renowned for their storytelling, how they conquered the villain and saved the day. In time, the story of Avalon would multiply. It would be reduced to nothing more than fairy tales, and historians would argue its authenticity for as long as mankind lived. The Dullahan's only concern was that of the Avalonians. He promised Nimue she would gain control, though he did not value that promise. It was simply empty words to pacify her. The truth was, he was still formulating his next step. That is until something unexpected fell into his lap.

While watching the other planets, his attention settled on Macha's former planet, where his creations remained imprisoned. The world began to shake uncontrollably until it exploded—chunks of the planet drifting out of the solar system. But as the planet was being destroyed, four balls of light soared from the planet's surface and flew toward Danu's planet. Intrigued, the Dullahan fixed his sight on Danu's world. There, he watched as his creations were being reprimanded by Danu. It didn't matter what was being said to them. What mattered was what happened next. Danu sent them away, and their spatial energies soared through space and even time, landing at the far reaches of another galaxy. He rotated his orb ever so slightly and checked surrounding galaxies until he landed on one in particular—one with an Earth. On a hunch, he scanned the world twice over and stopped as a tiny glow emanated from a land called England. He focused on the country to a city the humans called London. Here, in a small, quiet suburb, four figures emerged from a very expensive-looking building. The Dullahan's eyes widened as the figures looked a little perplexed, not with their surroundings, but it was as if they had awakened from a long slumber. These four looked nothing like the creatures he had created all those millennia ago. Still, their energy and magic were the exact same. He had no idea what memories were given to them or taken, but as he watched them go their separate ways, he could only think of one thing, "My new plan has only just begun."

WAR OF THE GODS

PART TWO

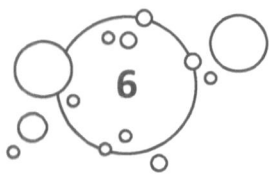

6

"It's still not working! Are you sure this is the right incantation?" whined Skylar, looking toward her teacher.

Merlin shook his head in irritation, "I am positive. Perhaps you need to enunciate your words."

"But I've been doing that for the last hour!"

Cameron looked at the pitiful situation and said, "You know, Merlin, she does have a point."

Merlin looked at the group of children, half of whom were lounging around on the grass. The youngest, Amethyst, seemed to be the only one perturbed by their mannerisms. She was the only one who had mastered the correct spell, and lately, she seemed to be as annoyed as Merlin.

"Morgan, please show them how to cast the spell?" Merlin asked as he rubbed his temples.

Wordlessly, the young girl walked in front of the children. Slowly and with some irritation, they turned their attention to her as she stretched her small arms, waved them clockwise, and suddenly transformed herself into a raven. In a flash of purple light, she turned back into her human form, adding an extra wave of her hand. The gesture indicating it was not that difficult.

"That's not fair," said Dakota, "She's an ancient sorceress and has much more time on us."

Merlin rolled his eyes and heaved a great sigh that made his long beard tremble, "Yes, I am aware of this matter. You all have been practicing this for weeks."

"In case you haven't noticed, we also just got back weeks ago. We didn't even have time to chill. We just dove right into magic school," snapped Ryder.

"The youth of these days," muttered Merlin to himself.

"Perhaps Ryder is right. Let us give them some time to rest, Merlin," reassured the youngest.

"So be it," said Merlin, disgruntled, "meet us here in one hour."

"An hour?" snapped Skylar.

"Two, and that is all I shall give."

The children nodded and headed toward the castle, leaving their little sister to speak with Merlin. None of them were used to this new Amethyst. It had only been a few months since they flew to Ireland and began their adventure. Shortly after, they discovered that Amethyst was never really Amethyst but the reincarnation of their direct ancestor, Morgan. When she started speaking in complete sentences and comprehending adult conversations, none of the children knew what to do with themselves. They had no time to process it, so they went with it. The fact she wanted to spend nearly all of her time with Merlin made the others feel as if they completely lost her or, rather, who they thought they knew.

As the group approached Camelot, they saw Conell talking with Avelia and Dillon, who appeared to be leaving. Judging by their embraces, the siblings appeared to be going away for a while. None of the kids seemed interested in getting involved. They all seemed too interested in finding a place to rest. As they walked the halls and made their way down toward their rooms, they passed Benji and two of his brothers as they rushed past them. For a moment, the kids turned to where they were going but collectively agreed that anything they were dealing with was not their problem. Although they liked Arthur, his other brothers were still unfamiliar to them.

"Uh oh," said Dakota as he came upon a dead end, "I think we're lost."

"Are you kidding me? Dude, we've been here long enough to not get lost!" exclaimed Ryder.

Skylar looked around the dead end and caught the light from the intriguing stained glass before them, "You know, Ryder makes a good point. We know our way around this place; we shouldn't have gotten lost...so why did we?"

They all looked around in silence until Cameron pointed out, "Hey, isn't the Relic Room supposed to be on the first floor by the library?"

Skylar stood mesmerized by the colors of the stained glass, "Yeah, why?"

"Uh, well, I know we climbed a few flights of stairs, so...why is it right here?"

The other three quickly turned to the room that Cameron pointed at and stared into the room. Objects stood neatly on their pedestals with a magical golden light shining down.

"Okay, I know this place is technically magical, but I'm pretty confident the floors and rooms don't move," Ryder said, looking around the room.

"Maybe we were led here?" asked Dakota doubtfully.

"I know Merlin wants us to learn that spell, but I think he's too busy talking with Amethyst...I mean Morgan. Besides, he isn't usually that sneaky," Skylar replied.

"So then, why are we here?" asked Ryder.

Skylar looked at him, then at her other brothers, and smiled slightly, "Let's find out!"

Together, they roamed the isles of various relics from times past. Each one was reverent and silent as they gazed at elements from their past. In between magic lessons, Merlin taught them in great detail what each item stood for and how they came to be so revered. There were staffs of various shapes and sizes, cauldrons, and more weapons than either of them could count. Occasionally, there'd be a pedestal with elements like the Holy Grail, but nothing truly stood out to them as bizarre until today.

Ryder passed by a gauntlet, one he had always admired before, but today, something stood to the left of it on the other side of the aisle. A large wooden double door stood in the shadows of the Relic Room. Moss crept up the sides of the dark wood, accenting the cracks in the ancient door. The brass handles appeared worn after years of use, but the ultimate question was who used them.

"Uh, guys, come take a look at this," Ryder called.

The others quickly came to their brother's side, and slowly, their confused expression matched Ryder's.

"Now, I know this isn't real," said Cameron, pointing a finger at the door, "We have been in this room hundreds of times since we got back from Avalon, and I know Merlin would have mentioned an additional room to the Relic Room."

"He would never miss a good educational moment, that's for sure," said Skylar.

Dakota looked at his watch and then went back to the door. "Well, we still have an hour and a half. Let's check it out!"

They started toward the mysterious room when the doors opened wide for them. The children hesitated, but upon peering into the room, they could see another set of pedestals with relics. But a periwinkle-colored light cascaded down on the few relics instead of a golden light like the others. Cautiously, they walked over the threshold and entered the room. Although they were intrigued by the relics, they felt something off with the room itself, and it had nothing to do with the low-lying fog rolling on the ground. This room felt more ancient than anything they'd ever come across.

"I don't think we're supposed to be in here," said Cameron as he circled the room slowly.

Skylar nodded, "Yeah, we should probably get out of here."

One by one, they started toward the exit when suddenly, the doors slammed shut on them, and the door frame became one with the wall. There was no way out. All of them looked around in panic.

"This is definitely *not* Merlin or Morgan. Something else is at work here," said Skylar.

"Could it be one of the fairies? Could they have followed us back?"

"What if Nimue is back? What if Moira didn't actually defeat her?"

Cameron quieted them down as he noticed the periwinkle light grew brighter on the pedestals, "I don't think it's either of those options, and I also don't think we'll be getting out of here until we do whatever it wants."

"And what's that? Stayed entombed in a creepy crypt?" asked Dakota.

Cameron pointed back to the relics, "I think we're in for another lesson. Wait, didn't Cerridwen mention something about a periwinkle light in her story? Something about another magical source? Could this be it? "

Skylar stepped back as the boys approached the pedestals, "Unlikely, that might be something strictly dealing with her. Besides, we're on Earth now, not Avalon. I'm starting to think we really shouldn't be here. Maybe the test is simpler than we think; maybe we actually have to find a way out?"

"What is it, Ryder?" asked Cameron out of the blue.

"I didn't say anything."

"You just called my name."

"No, you called mine!" Dakota piped up, his voice wavering slightly in concern.

They all stood silently until Skylar stared at the relic in front of her and said, "It's coming from them!"

They exchanged nervous glances as the calls got louder. Skylar stepped forward, nearly touching the relic in front of her, "All right, well, clearly this is what we need to do so; maybe if we all touch them at the same time, a door will open or something. Find the one that's calling your name."

She stepped in front of a large pedestal with what appeared to be a folded, tattered cloak. Cameron hesitantly approached a pedestal with a floating eyeball, and Dakota and Ryder were drawn to the same pedestal with a sword and shield set. The moment they all stood in place, the periwinkle light grew brighter and engulfed them as the scenes changed.

***

Dakota and Ryder suddenly found themselves in a bright green field. It appeared to be near dusk as the sun lit up the sky with an array of orange, yellow, and pink colors. Stars dotted the incoming night sky and met the sun's artistry with deep purples and blues. The boys looked around them to see if they could find anything that looked familiar, and although it seemed they were still in Ireland, it wasn't in an area they had ever seen.

"Skylar! Cameron!" called Dakota.

"They're not here, man," replied Ryder, defeated.

"No kidding," said Dakota, satisfied with his quick search, "maybe they're seeing something else. Our bodies could even still be in that room."

"Does it really matter?" asked Ryder as he started walking away from his brother.

"Dude, what's your problem? You've been this way for months," said Dakota, catching up to Ryder.

"Give it a rest. It doesn't matter."

"Yes, it does, we need you!"

"You sound an awful lot like we used to," came an unsuspecting voice.

The brothers quickly turned back where they had come and saw a massive rock slab they hadn't seen before. On it sat two men who looked nearly identical. Both wore heavy and well-used armor. The man to their left held a sword with its tip digging into the soft ground. He held his helmet underneath his other arm. He had long, vibrant red hair and deep brown eyes. His short red beard nearly covered everything but his bare chin, except for his long mustache, which hung well past his neck. He smiled at the boys and nodded as if reminiscing on the past. The man beside him held a shield close to his chest, revealing a simple bird engraved on it. The only difference with this man was his brown hair. Although it was long, he didn't share his friend's interest in facial hair. Instead, he sported two long sideburns. His smile was much more evident.

"Where did you come from?" asked Ryder, looking nervously at the sword.

"We could ask you the same thing," said the man with the sword, "We have always been here. It is you who have just arrived."

Dakota and Ryder exchanged confused looks. Dakota saw this as a puzzle, whether that was why they were there remained to be determined. "And why have we come here?"

"We are here to help you. After all, that *is* what spirit guides do," said the man with the shield.

"Spirit guides?" Ryder asked skeptically, "I already know who my spirit guides are."

"What is wrong with having more than one? Perhaps we have been communicating with the others," said the man with the sword as he stood up and sheathed it.

"For what purpose? To guide us? Where were you guys when we needed you in Avalon?" asked Ryder.

"My brother and I were not needed then. We are now," said the man with the shield, "Please, allow me to introduce ourselves. My name is Ennae and this here is my brother Berach."

"Uh, nice to meet you, I think," said Dakota.

"Look, we don't have time for this, we're supposed to meet back with our teacher in an hour. So, return the door or whatever it is you did," Ryder demanded.

The warrior brothers looked at each other and smiled. Then, they turned back to Ryder and Dakota, and Berach said, "Of course. We would like to show you something before you go, however. It may prove useful in your time."

Simultaneously, the brothers took their hands and grabbed at the atmosphere in front of them; like the ripples of a stage curtain, the horizon wrinkled, revealing a bright light in the center. The light seemed to crawl out of the opening, wiping away the fields before them.

The next moment reminded the boys much like that of a movie where the events were silent, but off camera, they could hear the voices of Berach and Ennae explaining the scenario. Two younger versions of Berach and Ennae ran around this massive throne room. They were as happy as can be as they seemed to be weaving in and out of this crowd of people. All were there to celebrate what appeared to be the crowning of a new king. This king stood in front of his throne and looked like a combination of the two boys. At first, Dakota and Ryder could only assume it to be their father, but when they noticed an older gentleman and his wife standing off to the side, each wearing a smaller crown, they thought again.

"That was at our oldest brother's coronation. He was such a great ruler of that time. Even our father once said that Fergus would rule the world if given the chance," came Berach's voice.

The children ran to their brother's side as he hugged them both. He then made his way through the crowd, greeting all his new subjects with a smile. The people returned a smile. King Fergus left the room with his family and people following after. He walked to a set of doors which magically opened for him. He stepped onto a balcony where the rest of Camelot stood below, cheering on their new ruler.

"The kingdom was happy for a time—prosperous even. The fairies would not have that, though," said Ennae sadly. The scene before the boys changed to a somber time where warriors and fairies fought against each other, "As you can see, it was a losing battle on our side. We had magic. At least, the royal family did, but it was nothing compared to the fairies."

A group of weary warriors tumbled into the courtyard. Two men removed their helmets, revealing an older version of the jubilant boys in the previous vision. Their spirits were as low as their stamina. They sat by a fairly large well on the ground and drank from the full bucket on the edge.

"It was hopeless. That is what it felt like for decades. Fergus' excitement for the throne soon became a burden," said Berach as the scene fell upon an older Fergus who sat on the throne with his head in his hands. His golden crown shifted haphazardly on his head, "But it was not entirely his fault."

A montage of scenes flew before them, mostly showing Berach and Ennae enjoying life to the fullest. Whether it be drinking in the nearest tavern or living it up at Camelot's many parties; as they grew older, they drew farther away from the castle and their responsibilities. With Fergus in charge, the brothers no longer felt they needed to attend court as much.

"You see, the problem was, Fergus lost hope because we fell so far from our court duties. We thought the land was perfect and nothing could go wrong. The fairies knew this and saw a perfect opportunity to attack," said Ennae as the scene went to Fergus in front of a war table—his appearance disheveled. "To make a sad and long story short, Fergus abdicated the throne. And although Berach and I had the rightful claim, we ran away. We felt we were not fit to rule.

So, our cousin Elisedd rose to power. He was the patriarch of King Arthur's line. And he made just as good a ruler as Fergus."

That same blinding light flashed in front of them again, returning them to the same fields. The brothers sat back on their rock as before, but their expressions were sorrowful.

Dakota and Ryder looked at each other in confusion until Ryder said, "So what was the point of that?"

Berach sighed, "You and Dakota are not too different from us. We lost that battle with the fairies and many others because we made a mistake. We thought our brother could control everything, but, in truth, our kingdom fell because we did not help him. We did not see our value until it was too late."

"Look, our sister isn't a queen, and we are far from royalty," said Dakota with a small laugh.

"But do you see your value to her and Cameron?" Ennae prodded, "You are in the midst of the greatest battle this solar system has ever seen. And you are what holds your family together."

"How?" Dakota and Ryder asked together, each looking at the other doubtfully.

"You two are the lights in their life. The reason why they fight so hard to have a safe life. You have not endured the pain they have. You must support and protect them," said Berach, almost pleadingly.

Dakota narrowed his eyes suspiciously, "You're not really our spirit guides, are you?"

A wide smile stretched across the warriors' faces as Berach replied, "Now, that is a fascinating question. But it's not our story to tell. I suppose you will just have to wait."

***

Skylar and Cameron's situation was similar to that of their little brothers. However, their spirit guides were not. Skylar found herself on a dry patch of land in a misty bog. The sky was overcast, and the thick fog only added to the dreary atmosphere. Suddenly, the land around her grew loud with the rustle of dead trees and the sloshing of murky water. Out from the fog stepped pale feet, followed by a ratty cloaked figure. It stopped two feet from Skylar as it took its scrawny hands and drew back its hood, revealing an old woman with white hair that cascaded down her back. Her skin appeared sallow—even deathlike. Her pale blue eyes nearly blended in with her skin. She reached out her hand and snatched Skylar's hand in hers. For a moment, all was black until the woman began showing her images. No words followed, like Berach and Ennae, but it wasn't needed.

As the woman began telling Skylar her story, the young witch started to understand who the silent woman was. Her name was Clíodhna, and she wasn't always the scary woman she portrayed. She used to be the queen of the banshees, an ancient group of women who cared for those near their deaths. They would announce their presence with a horrible cry in the night. To many, they were an angel of mercy, but the banshees were looked down upon when they started calling on those who the people deemed too young to die. Clíodhna attempted to calm the people's fears, but that only led to more hatred. She felt sorrow for the pain she caused but knew that it was not her fault. She was gifted by the gods, and so were her people. This was her calling.

Tears fell from Skylar's eyes when the scene returned to the bog. She knew exactly why she saw that. "Now I understand," was all she could utter.

A wrinkled smile grew on the old woman's face as she placed her hood up and returned to the fog.

***

Cameron's story took place on a battlefield. Carnage was all around him as his guide was in front of him; his sword pointed to the sky in victory. The warrior's men gathered around him in triumph. Cameron stood still; never had he seen so much death, but he also felt so much joy through the man before him. He walked toward Cameron; he rested his sword against his burly shoulder, leaving a trail of dripping blood in his path.

"Ah, you must be my charge, and I am your spirit guide." said that man proudly, "I am Balor, warrior King, or I was, centuries ago. In fact, I was the first king among the first people created on Avalon. This you see here is but a minor skirmish."

"You call this minor?" asked Cameron nervously.

"Indeed I do," said Balor as his men wandered off into the blood-red sky, "I have faced many foes—some were even, dare I say, friends."

Cameron averted his gaze from the burly man. He knew that feeling of betrayal all too well. But, Balor continued, his lips curved into a smile, "I was around your age when I experienced my first heartbreak. I do not mean love. I mean—well, let me show you."

With a gentle wave of his hand, the scene before him changed. They were in a large room with a table stretching its length. A massive meal was prepared for the group sitting on each side. It appeared to be a celebration of sorts, as everyone was chatting merrily and clanking together goblets with cheer. At the head of the table sat a younger version of Balor. If Cameron had to guess, he assumed the feast was for a new king. Although the man to his right looked anything but pleased.

"That disgruntled man was my younger brother, Oisin," said Balor as the scene focused on the seated man. He looked almost identical to Balor, except he wasn't as muscular, "He always stood by my side and even gave me great counsel during times of war. Regretfully, he started listening to people who poisoned his mind against me.

The scene changed to a shady-looking man whispering in Oisin's ear. He nodded as his eyebrows furrowed in anger. He stormed away from his informant, and the scene swiftly moved to a more pleasant one where he was laughing with Balor, "I would be lying if I said I did not suspect my brother of betraying me. I knew who he was speaking with, and I knew his tells of paranoia. I was in denial. I wanted to believe the best. I found where his true loyalties lay during one evening when my army was taken by surprise."

A battlefield stood before Cameron, tents stood tall, and the smoke from various fireplaces reached all the way to the sky, obscuring the stars. Men in partial armor walked around. Some even entered their tents to relax for the night.

The majority of the tents were unlit—signifying those who chose to turn in early. A few men decided to stay up around the fires, regaling their friends with stories, though few smiled. Suddenly, a stream of fireballs lit up the night sky and cascaded down upon the sleeping camp one by one. Within five minutes, the once peaceful camp was filled with blood and carnage. Balor came tumbling out of a fiery tent and landed at Oisin's feet, who looked down on him with hatred. Trembling from the sudden attack, Balor looked up at his assailant. With a jab of his dagger, Oisin plunged the blade into Balor's eye, and with a quick swish of the weapon, it rolled into the palm of his hand. Balor covered his bloodied eye socket in pain as Oisin held up the eye like a trophy. He let out a loud, booming laugh as the scene before Cameron faded away, returning him to the battlefield.

"As you can see," said Balor, sheathing his sword, "you and I have much in common."

"How do you figure?" asked Cameron.

"We both thought we could trust the one we were supposed to trust—family. I trusted my brother, and you trusted your father."

Cameron stepped back, "How...how could you know that? Oh, right, spirit guide. Well, he lied to me, and my mom ended up dead."

"And you blame yourself; you feel that you failed," Balor replied sympathetically, "but he failed you. You tried to stop him—make him see reason. You cannot reason with someone who refuses to see the error of their own ways."

"I know that now, a bit too late, though," replied Cameron solemnly.

"Perhaps not; perhaps you know just when you are meant to," Balor replied with a smile.

"You're not a typical spirit guide, are you?"

"Not even close," Balor's voice echoed as he disappeared.

***

The children found themselves back in the mysterious room once more. They glanced at each other silently, all wondering what the others witnessed. Faded tear stains graced Skylar's cheek, which she promptly brushed away. Ryder and Dakota gave each other a smile of understanding, and Cameron simply stared at the relic floating before him. By the time they got their bearings, all of the relics glowed simultaneously, and they quickly enveloped their humans. Everyone covered their eyes as the glow grew brighter, encompassing the entire room. Just as soon as it came, it suddenly left.

As the children adjusted their eyes to the new lighting, they noticed they were back in the regular Relic Room outside the mysterious side room. Dakota was the first to see the location change, "The door's gone."

The wall to the side looked exactly as before the door opened. Cameron looked from the wall to his siblings and said, "What was that?"

Skylar opened her mouth to give her idea when Ryder held out his wrist, "Um, guys...better question. What's *this*?"

Displayed on Ryder's right wrist was what appeared to be a tattoo of the triquetra that was a forest green in color. Dakota came up to his side and held up his left wrist. Cameron and Skylar checked theirs only to find their wrists bare of any mark. They looked at each other, and their mouths opened slightly in shock. Skylar pointed at Cameron's shoulder, and she pulled back his shirt sleeve to reveal the mark. In turn, he pointed to his neck, signaling to Skylar that hers had also appeared. Skylar rushed to a nearby relic that had a reflective surface and examined her neck. She rubbed the strange mark to be sure that it was real.

Still staring at her reflection, she put her hand down and replied, "I think it's time we talk to Merlin."

Thankful that the castle wasn't playing tricks on them this time, the kids managed to make it out of the castle at record speed. They rushed through the field toward where they last left their master. Amethyst was still speaking to Merlin when all four of the children nearly collapsed at their feet.

Cameron was the first to look up at Merlin. The old man looked down on all of them with a concerned expression. But it was Amethyst who started the conversation. She walked over to Skylar, placed her small hand on the mark, and gasped.

She looked up at Merlin and said in awe, "Brother, it is the Anam Léirigh!"

Merlin's curious face turned to shock quickly as he watched the other three reveal their mark. He locked his gaze with Cameron for a moment and touched the mark on Cameron's shoulder, "That...that is impossible!"

"What's not possible?" asked Cameron.

Merlin shook himself from his stupor and sat down on the ground with the children. Amethyst parked herself right by Skylar and put her hand on her shoulder in comfort as Merlin began his story.

"That is the mark of Anam Léirigh. It loosely translates to Soul Manifest. It is an ancient spell far older than me or Morgan. Until now, I believed it to be a story parents told their children. A story that brought hope to all. The origins are a little uncertain, depending on who you ask. However, one thing everyone knew. If you received the mark, you were destined to be a hero among men."

Amethyst piped up, "Recite the incantation, and let us see what gifts you received."

The other children exchanged nervous glances and then simultaneously said the phrase. The tattoos on their bodies glowed, and weapons manifested before them in various forms. Ryder held a transparent shield with the same colored glow as the tattoo, and Dakota wielded a matching sword. They both looked at each other, and a smile formed on their faces, remembering their adventure in that strange memory. Cameron's weapon was far more sinister. He rubbed his eyes, trying to get something out of them. When he opened them, one eye had a strange red glint that grew as he focused. In a snap, a red laser came out of the eyes and split a nearby rock in half. Skylar's power was much more noticeable. A scraggly cloak billowed around her, and her hair was now white and wild. She opened her mouth to speak, but a blood-curdling scream was all that emerged. She quickly covered her mouth as she noticed the others around her covered their ears.

For a brief moment, the children felt confident in their newfound gift and secure in the coming storm. Even Amethyst looked happy until her eyes caught something on the distant horizon. Her tiny eyebrows furrowed as she focused on the anomaly, "Do...do you see that?"

The others quickly turned to where she was looking. Fear replaced their joyous expressions as Merlin said, "It is time...the battle has begun."

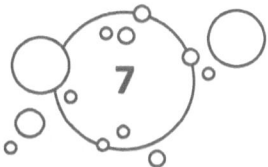

7

A kick—a slight but simple tug. Had her round stomach not been covering the view of her feet, Avelia would have thought it to be her muscles flinching, but the last several months have proved this not to be true. She touched her stomach gently, looking up at the castle she grew to love.

Camelot towered over her—its spires reaching so high it was a wonder more Earthlings didn't stop to stare at its magnificence.

"Avelia," Dillon's voice called gently. Avelia felt his presence stop beside her. He lovingly wrapped an arm around her in comfort. "We need to go."

"How can we leave them like this?" she asked as a tear streamed down her face.

"My magic is mediocre at best, and you are in no condition to fight an inter-spacial battle."

Avelia released a quiet chuckle and nodded her head. With one last glimpse of Camelot, she turned away for the last time. She started walking away from the castle and noticed, to her left, that the children and Merlin were busy practicing an elaborate spell—though the children seemed to have lost interest as a few had already taken rest on the ground. But they weren't her destination—that lay on the other side of the grounds where a car sat waiting. A tall, slender man stood to the side, holding a door open. Her heart leaped in her chest at Conall's presence. And for the first time in days, she smiled. But, as she drew nearer to the car, she could easily see that he didn't meet her emotion. In fact, he looked just as he had the day he found out he was not Camelot's heir. Avelia held her hands out to take his as she reached the car. He accepted gingerly and with a silent tear escaping his eye.

"I don't have to leave; I can stay here and fight. History is full of women warriors, and I doubt any of them stopped fighting for their freedom because of pregnancy," Avelia pleaded.

"But did any of those battles involve magic, let alone magic from another world?" Conall rebutted.

Avelia pouted slightly, "It still isn't right, I must help! It wouldn't be right for me to leave you all like this. I'm Camelot's ruler, for Heaven's sake!"

Conall's grip tightened, "This is not up for debate, Avelia. I will not let you put yourself in harm's way, especially when carrying the next generation of Avalonians!"

Avelia's eyebrows furrowed as she struggled to hold back a wave of tears. She straightened herself up as best she could and replied, "Fine, the same goes for you. If I can't take part in this battle, then neither shall you. Our child needs a father. I don't care about the circumstances surrounding the start of the battle, but you will be far from it and safe. Is that clear?"

Conall looked to Dillon for assistance, but he just stared at his sister, dumbfounded by her command. To any outsider, this would seem like a typical couple's quarrel. But to the Avalonians, this was far more serious and dangerous. An ancient curse that began with the patriarch of Conall's line—Mordred. He failed in his duties to protect the crown of Camelot, and in doing so, Morgan made sure that his line would have no choice but to serve the rulers of Camelot. No one knew what occurred the last time one from Conall's line disobeyed a direct order—they only heard rumors of an unpleasant, magical death. Conall had never experienced anything by way of an order, and Avelia had always been careful with her wording whenever she asked him to do something for her.

Avelia's stern gaze seemed to penetrate Conall. He tore his attention away from her for a brief moment and noticed the children walking up to the castle—their heads hanging low. He dropped his shoulders, silently conceding to Avelia's demand. She raised her hand to his cheek, and her expression softened, "I'm so sorry, Conall. You didn't give me a choice."

He wordlessly nodded as she slowly got into the car. Before closing the door, he leaned down and quietly said, "I still love you."

A tear streamed down her face. She knew this phrase all too well. Over the last year and a half of being tormented by Nimue and battling forces from other worlds, that phrase reminded both parties that their love would endure. She gave him a weak smile as he closed the door.

***

Conall looked up at Dillon and shook his hand; neither exchanged a word, just a nod of understanding. As Dillon climbed into the driver's seat and turned on the car, Conall walked away toward the castle—his hands in his pockets. As he reached the castle, the grand doors flew open, and a group of servants exited. They chatted happily with each other but slowly stopped their gabbing when Conall walked past. He gave them a polite smile, but sour expressions were all he received. He turned away and entered the castle with his head hung low. That was the typical greeting he always expected from the servants and other royal court members. He was just grateful that the children, Merlin, and Amethyst had never reacted this way toward him. He supposed it was because they had gone through so much together. The servants and other nobles wouldn't understand the bond they had.

Still, in his mind, he thought he deserved at least some form of forgiveness from everyone he was unkind towards. He was a changed man; sure, it was a relatively new leaf. But those who hated him didn't give him a chance.

Conall slipped by a few more glaring servants and escaped into the library. He closed the heavy wooden doors and leaned against them, breathing in the musty smell of the old paper. Books from all parts of Camelot's history lined the walls, along with books from Earth. A tremendous round stone table sat in the middle of the room where he and the others met with Moira's evil kidnapper, Malachi. Although that time was not long ago, it felt like a lifetime in many ways. Conall walked along the walls, brushing his fingertips across the fragile book covers. Despite the conversations in this room, he found solace here. Its silence and solitude were probably why he saw this as his favorite room in the castle. He walked along the bookshelf-lined walls and brushed his fingers along the dusty old bindings. Heaving a heavy sigh, Conall turned toward the table in the center of the room. As he turned, a heavy book fell from its resting spot and slammed on the stone ground. Conall jumped and slammed against another bookshelf as several books followed their friend to the ground. Conall threw his hands up in defeat and uttered a few choice words—not even the books agreed with him, it seemed.

A few unusual books caught his attention as he bent down to pick up the literary carnage. Unlike the others in the room, these had no titles, and the covers seemed to be made of ancient bindings, the likes of which he hadn't even seen in the Relic Room. Ignoring the other books on the ground, he put the others on the table and spread them out. One by one, he carefully opened the covers. He saw they all described the legends regarding Mordred and his family's curse. Blindly, he reached for a chair to settle himself in until he heard a door slam shut in the hallway. Startled, he haphazardly grabbed the books and rushed out the door—catching sight of the kids as they walked down the hall toward him.

He didn't know where to go. Sure, he had a room at the castle, but it wasn't private enough for the information he was about to delve into. No, he needed to find a place he had control over, and that wasn't Camelot. Conall raced to the entrance and threw open the doors, making a beeline for his car. He'd only be gone for a few hours; at least, that's what he told himself. Besides, where he was going wasn't that far. Calmly, he pulled the car out of the driveway and drove down the road to the only real home he knew now—Wolfe Castle.

***

He rolled up to the decaying structure, taking in the ivory colored covered walls. He parked the car and exited—

immediately stepping on glass shards from forgotten window panes. Graffiti in all designs and colors loudly stretched across the walls as far as the vandals could go. Conall heaved a heavy sigh as he stepped across the threshold of his former home, a now constant reminder of everything he lost.

With each step, his footsteps echoed off the walls, adding a haunting ambiance to the empty halls. The artists who painted the castle's exterior didn't just leave their signatures; they took everything they could carry. Whatever they couldn't, they smashed to pieces for fun. He made his way up a flight of winding stairs and found his way to his old study. He winced as he grabbed the door handle—afraid of what disaster awaited him on the other side.

The door swung open with ease, and Conall was met with a pleasant surprise. His desk stood in the center of the room, and a vintage lamp sat on the edge flickering on and off. Papers were strewn about, ready to be read or signed, and a reference book sat haphazardly off to the side—threatening to fall off at the slightest breeze. It was exactly how he left it. As he neared his desk, a gust of warm air engulfed his side. He stopped and turned to see a roaring fire burning in the fireplace. His eyebrows furrowed; it hadn't been lit a moment before. He continued to his desk, where he pulled out a large, green felted chair and sat down. He pushed around the papers, curious as to what he left forgotten. His right hand brushed across the table, nearly knocking over a small tumbler. He caught it from tipping over the edge as brown liquid escaped the glass, spilling onto the mahogany desk. Yet again, his eyebrows furrowed in confusion as beside the tumbler sat a decanter half-full of whiskey. He looked around, wondering if someone was hiding in the shadows and having fun with him. He lifted the tumbler to his nose when the dark corners revealed nothing. He gathered a whiff of the contents and smiled. It was his favorite brand.

He tilted the cup back and let the alcohol warm his body. The fire blew out as he finished the last drop, and the desk and tumbler vanished. He quickly stood up. His chair had disappeared, too. The only thing remaining in the room was the ghost of a fire in the fireplace—its embers still glowing.

Smoke billowed around him, and the only light source was through a few cracks in the boarded-up window behind him. Suddenly, the smoke started taking form and swarmed around him synchronized, coming to a stop in front of him. Conall squinted his eyes as the smoke shaped itself into a dragon's head. The form opened its mouth and breathed hot air onto Conall's face before dispersing.

"Dragon magic, of course," Conall whispered, his voice reverberating off the walls. He started for the hall as he continued, "It seems I can't get away from it."

As he stepped out of the room, he jumped back when he saw a glowing spectral form appear in front of him. It seemed to have heard his comment as it replied, "And why would you want to?"

He stared at the figure before him, not entirely surprised. Spirits and magic weren't exactly mutually exclusive in his mind. But he knew this entity all too well.

He rolled his eyes and sighed in defeat, "Grandfather, of course it'd be you to come to me. Seems I also can't escape you."

The figure fully formed into an older man with black, graying hair and a stern look. He stood tall but was slightly hunched over due to the cane he leaned against. The stiff suit he wore seemed to make his movements even more restricted than his old age.

"I see. Even after all these years, your opinion of me has not changed," said the man with a slight chuckle. His lips curved into a smile, increasing the wrinkles on his long face.

"I grew up with your constant harassment. It was always about carrying on the family legacy. What legacy? It wasn't even ours to begin with!" Conall said, becoming more agitated.

The old man began to shift uncomfortably. He took his cane and leaned on it with both hands, leaning in towards his grandson, "And I was wrong; all of your ancestors were wrong."

"Wow, all it took was for you to die to admit you were wrong. Why take that long?"

"In truth, none of us knew our ancestral origin story until

we passed. In the spirit realm, we can communicate with all of our ancestors from the beginning of time." said his grandfather solemnly.

Conall stared into space, processing this information, "Wait, but the spirits are free to move about this world and Avalon. I don't understand why no one reached out to us. So many things could have been avoided if we knew the truth!"

"The spirit world is a bit more complicated than that," said the old man. "We are always able to watch over our loved ones and descendants, but communicating with them is difficult. Oftentimes, it takes a tragedy or horrific event for us to cross into this plain and speak with you. Other times—well, it only takes a little magic."

Conall frowned at his grandfather, "But I wasn't using any magic. I was just looking for a quiet place to collect my thoughts."

"My dear grandson, you are from Avalon. Magic isn't just an incantation. It's part of your very being! In that brief moment of silence, you were calling out for someone to hear you."

Conall shook his head, "I wasn't calling out for you."

"You are right," the old man stepped aside, and with a wave of his hand, a portal appeared off to his left, "I am merely a messenger."

Conall shifted his gaze to the portal where dragons flew around a floating island. The image beyond the portal seemed to move on its own accord. It zoomed in past the smaller dragons into the island, where the dragon god Sly stood tall, staring directly into the portal at Conall, his gaze piercing through his soul. The dragon curled his massive wings around him like a regal cloak. Conall stepped forward, almost entranced by the dragon's glare.

He stopped abruptly and shook his head as if trying to rid himself of a terrible thought. He turned his attention back to his grandfather, "No, there's nothing the dragons can do for me. They don't care about human squabbles."

"Ah, your situation isn't just an ordinary squabble, My Boy. Everyone's fate lies in the outcome of this galactic battle—the dragons included," the old man said with a twinkle in his eye, "Perhaps you can assist each other."

Conall turned his head toward his desk and saw a dust-covered picture frame still standing—the only thing in the entire building that vandals had never touched. He walked toward it and gingerly picked up the frame. He blew off the dust to reveal a picture of him and Avelia. It was taken at a time in his life before Camelot, before the magic was known—a happier time. For a brief moment, he felt happiness until the thoughts of the present started to creep back in. Avelia ordered him not to fight—an order he was compelled to follow. A surge of rage overcame him as he tossed the picture onto the desk and spun back toward the portal. He had already lost so much from this war—he wasn't about to lose Avelia and his unborn child.

With a furrowed brow and a commanding voice, he said, "Get me an audience with the Dragon God."

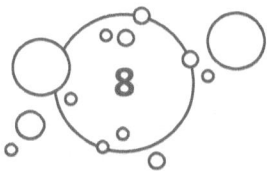

8

"Mother should be attending this meeting," Brigid said softly.

"I believe, Dear Sister, that is the reason for her absence," Morrighan retorted.

"I concur. She should have a say in this matter," echoed Caer Ibormeith.

The gods had been in their usual meeting location, a small moon near the center of the solar system. It was always considered a mutual ground where everyone had a voice—even the darker deities. A massive table sat in the middle of a marble-like floor, with four marble pillars standing at the four corners.

There were no walls in this location, just near and distant stars and planets rotating around them. Typically, these meetings included the Mother at the head of the table where Cerridwen now sat. The meetings consisted of her rambling about what they were doing wrong—except for her favorite children. But this time, the meeting was without her, and many chairs also sat vacant. This meeting had lasted for hours if not days. Cerridwen couldn't be sure about the exact time, but it was the most exhausting meeting she had ever attended. Nothing was getting accomplished aside from the general discussion of the ensuing battle. To which, no one could still agree.

Morrighan and Arwn were ready to fight, as expected, but the other, more benign entities weren't so convinced this was their fight. Dagda seemed to be the only one of the gentler gods willing to consider both sides. As for Brigid and Caer, it was anyone's guess as to why they were even there. Neither Cernunnos nor Cailleach even bothered to show. Aengus and Lugos lasted the first hour and then began arguing about who was the better deity. Belenus stayed only out of spite for the Mother, but he didn't seem to care much.

He was mainly feasting on the rumors about the Mother's lies.

"The Mother's actions aside, we still have a problem on our hands. How are we to handle this—Dullahan creature?" asked Dagda, brushing off the two goddesses.

"The Avalonians are practicing their magic and getting stronger by the day. I believe the young gods are also trying to sort through some special spells. They think they can outwit their creator," Cerridwen replied, relaying the information as best she could.

"I admire your optimism and unwavering trust in these Avalonians, but their magic is no match for the Dullahan, and as for his creations, how do you know they are not still working for him?" asked Morrighan, her tone a little less condescending than usual.

Cerridwen looked taken aback by Morrighan's response. She looked downcast as she replied, "I...I cannot speak for the young gods, but the Avalonians' lives are at stake, as are ours. We will be prisoners if we allow this Dullahan to take over our worlds. We must fight back before it's too late."

"And what do you consider is too late?" asked Belenus, trying to pretend to be part of the conversation.

"When our worlds no longer resemble us. I am telling you the truth. It is only a matter of time before this happens. We must act now!" Cerridwen snapped.

"And what do you propose we do? Take on this thing ourselves? Confront the Dullahan with just our will? If he is as strong as you say, no one stands a chance against him. Just let it be. You say he has grief with Mother. I do not see why she cannot take care of it," said Caer Ibormeith.

"That's the point now, isn't it. No one has seen Mother, and I'm sure she would be at this meeting already," said Arwn. "Morrighan and I have seen what he can do. He is a threat, to be sure, and he isn't one that Mother can handle."

"Arwn! Enough!" Morrighan scolded.

"I thought you didn't know anything about the Dullahan," said Cerridwen, staring at Morrighan, waiting for an answer.

Morrighan gave Arwn a warning look. Arwn, in turn, looked down at the table, knowing he'd be punished for his outburst later. The goddess turned her threatening gaze onto Cerridwen, who was having difficulty understanding the emotions behind her dark eyes. If there was anything she could interpret, it was an overwhelming sense of fear—an uncommon emotion with Morrighan.

"I am sorry, but this sounds like sibling disputes and nothing that concerns me or Brigid. I think we ought to take our leave now. Should you need us for anything *else*, you may call for us."

Caer Ibormeith and Brigid rose from the table simultaneously and disappeared in a cloud of smoke. Their expressions as they disappeared were nothing but disdain. Cerridwen rolled her eyes at their response, but in her mind, it was probably best they left.

"Well, that became quite awkward rather quickly, I think I shall take my leave too. But do keep me informed if the Mother has made any more tantalizing transgressions. It is my only entertainment these days," said Belenus as he, too, disappeared back into his world.

Cerridwen then looked to the last other deity remaining—Dagda. "Would you care to leave as well?"

The god looked between his brother and sisters, his bushy eyebrows furrowed with this new information, "No, please proceed. Morrighan, I am rather intrigued by all of this."

Morrighan looked at Dagda and Cerridwen, both unwilling to let Arwn's slip-up go. The goddess sighed heavily, "We—we had one interaction with him while on Macha's planet. But we didn't know who or what he is. She never explained, he did most of the talking."

"Unfortunately, we never spoke or saw them after that brief visit. If we did, we would have been more forthcoming about our information," Arwn chimed in.

"Would you, though? You have never been forthcoming about anything unless it suits you," Cerridwen challenged.

"Well, I would say that considering the circumstances, this suits me, Sister," Morrighan threatened. "Besides, what does it matter now? Even if we had the information, I sincerely doubt it would help when we first spoke about the Dullahan. We still didn't have all the information."

"Let us stop dwelling on the past and focus on the present. Tell us all you know," said Dagda, fully immersed in the conversation.

Morrighan shifted uncomfortably in her chair. The ravens perched on her shoulders moved with her as if they were alive. She heaved a heavy sigh as if revealing her deepest secret, "Macha is still alive."

"But I thought you said her planet was dest—" started Cerridwen.

"Yes, it was destroyed, but a part of her remains alive," Morrighan interrupted, "A part of her soul remains that is. How? I can't say, but I have heard her whispering on the winds of my planet."

Cerridwen exchanged uncertain looks with Dagda, who only shook his head as if responding to Cerridwen's ensuing question. She looked back at Morrighan and replied, "We haven't heard any whispers, Morrighan."

"You wouldn't. She only ever comes to me," Morrighan said solemnly as she looked down in her lap. She relaxes her position and then looks back up at Dagda and Cerridwen, "She is my love."

"Uh, your...I thought Arwn and you—" started Dagda. Cerridwen opened her mouth to continue his thought, "What he means is..."

Morrighan and Arwn looked confused at their siblings and then looked at each other. They suddenly burst out laughing upon realizing what they were implying. Arwn spoke up after wiping away a stray tear, "Hardly! We are what you'd consider *special* friends. There is nothing truly romantic between us."

Morrighan piped in, "It is merely an occasional—fling. Macha and I had a fierce—disagreement centuries before the Dullahan's arrival. Afterwards, Arwn became my closest ally. He was the only one who knew of our love. I confided in him, and he even tried to help me locate her soul, but we were not powerful enough to obtain it ourselves."

"I think it is an admirable feat, trying to locate her. But, not to be rude, how do you suppose finding her will help us with the Dullahan?" asked Cerridwen delicately.

"Because Macha knows his weakness. I can grasp words and sometimes phrases among her whispers. What I've surmised is that he has one. I must go to her and bring her soul back. Arwn and I nearly reached her at one point, but we need more magic to leave our solar system."

Cerridwen rose in shock, panicking, "*Leave the solar system? Are* you out of your mind? What would happen to your planet?"

"Calm yourself. I'm not truly leaving my planet. I'm just projecting myself. I can still touch things and walk among the living. It's as if I'm in two places at once, although should anyone see me, I'd appear as a spirit. But I have never been able to last longer than a few hours—not enough time to find her. Perhaps you can help. You have traveled among our planets; maybe you will find it easier?"

Cerridwen locked her gaze with Morrighan, expecting her to give a clue that she was lying about everything. But she didn't even blink—not even a twitch in her eyes. She was dead serious; at the very least, she believed everything she was saying. Cerridwen's gaze turned to Arwn, who looked at Morrighan almost longingly. He truly did love her in his own twisted way. Maybe not in a romantic way, but he certainly cared about Morrighan's feelings. Cerridwen could feel Dagda's eyes on her. She didn't have to look at him to know what he was thinking. *Are you seriously considering this?* Yes, she was. If there was a slight chance that Macha was alive, she might even know more about the Dullahan. It was a risk Cerridwen was willing to take, considering the odds were stacked high against them.

"All right, how do I do this?" she asked in resignation.

For the first time in Cerridwen's life, she witnessed a sincere smile stretch across Morrighan's face. She wasn't even aware the goddess knew how to do that. That's how she knew Morrighan was being honest about everything. Morrighan stretched out her hand toward Cerridwen across the table. Hesitantly, the goddess accepted, and within seconds, the world around her faded into darkness.

***

Ugh, she could not have warned me how uncomfortable the transition was? Cerridwen thought as she landed on a dark planet similar to Morrighan's. But it wasn't the same; this land was nearly entirely barren, except for a distant forest. It was unlike any forest she had ever seen. The trees were tall with long, spindly branches that appeared as if they were waiting for their next victim. The ground beneath her feet was dry, and a strange purple hue surrounded her. The only light came from a distant planet with a golden aura. It felt as if the only heat came from that as well. *Such a desolate place,* Cerridwen pondered as she started to walk about the land. Her projected form felt strange, and she remembered how it had begun.

Morrighan reached across the table and brought her to her land. The process was almost instantaneous as if they knew she'd agree to Morrighan's request. Arwn took Cerridwen's hand, and Morrighan held onto her other hand. Together, they chanted some ancient celestial spell, and Cerridwen felt herself become light as smoke, but it wasn't without a slight twinge of pain. With every inch her projection stepped away from them, she felt a slight pull as if her body knew this wasn't a natural spell, but one Arwn and Morrighan had created over the centuries in their attempts at finding Macha. She had no way of contacting them, which made this search all the more difficult. Only Morrighan had heard Macha's soul; how would Cerridwen know what to listen for? For all she knew, Macha's soul sounded like her voice—gurgling and always challenging to understand.

Cerridwen rolled her eyes as she made her way deeper into the planet. She listened for any sound to indicate Macha, but all that came were the sounds of distant wild animals. She sighed, prepared to give up at any moment, but a loud explosion echoed in her ear just as that thought crossed her mind. The blast was followed by more minor explosions as if someone were trying to create a distraction. A cloud of smoke emerged from the tree line ahead. She swiftly approached the anomaly flying high over the trees and through the smoke. Below, she could see two figures running away, but as she looked around, she could see no one chasing after them. She was about to fly onward when she caught the sound of a whisper, a familiar gurgling whisper.

Help me! Came a weak voice.

Cerridwen spun around toward the fleeting figures and started to follow them—keeping a safe distance from being seen.

Please help me! The voice continued to echo. *I am trying. Please hold on!* Cerridwen tried to reply, though her voice echoed just as much, and it was probably drowned out by the wind. She had to keep following. When the figures stopped, Cerridwen was hovering over a relatively large village. Hundreds of people went about their day doing chores and having deep discussions with other villagers. But these weren't ordinary people—they had ancient and powerful magic. A magical boundary line surrounded this village, preventing something from entering. She looked around her but could only see a dark city miles away. *Who could they be guarding themselves from?* She wondered. She floated closer into the village and saw more people using magic; some used ancient incantations, much like the three children used when practicing with Merlin. But none of these humans had the blood of Avalonians. So, who exactly were they? Cerridwen assumed that Avalonians were the only ones to possess magic, but she was in another galaxy across the universe; anything was possible.

Suddenly, her attention was redirected to the two figures she was following. A man and a young woman were walking into camp. The man seemed to know where he was going; the young woman, on the other hand, looked confused and lost, maybe even a little fearful, but she hid that rather well. *Help me!* The voice came, and this time, it almost shouted. Cerridwen's eyes darted to the girl. She hadn't spoken those words, and that's when the goddess focus zoomed in on the girl's hand where a medium sized ring with a burnt auburn stone in the center wrapped snugly around her finger. *Macha? Is that you?* Cerridwen called out.

The girl stopped suddenly and looked around, almost as if she heard Cerridwen, but that was impossible. Cerridwen was in such a form that hardly anyone, human or deity, could identify her. All the same, she decided to be even more careful. She sensed this young woman had powerful magic, more potent than the entirety of this village. This type of magic she was unfamiliar with. The young woman began watching the others around her cast spells. She pulled off the ring and began speaking with her guide. They seemed to be talking about the ring. She looked disappointed. Something had happened to the ring; it either wasn't what she wanted or broke. Cerridwen couldn't quite read her lips. Regardless of the reason, the guide called out to a nearby villager. After a few words, the young woman relinquished her ownership of the ring.

The villager walked away, and it was Cerridwen's cue to follow. She floated down behind a makeshift tent, which appeared to be the villager's home. Cerridwen peered around the corner to see the female place the ring on a table before entering her home. She could hear the woman puttering around in her tent, seemingly looking for something long forgotten. Cerridwen sneaked around the corner and shifted her projection stealthily toward the ring. She gingerly lifted the ring to her face as she stared into the center of the ring. She could see a faint flicker of light, a reminder that Macha was still there.

Macha, Morrighan was right. You are still alive!

A loud gasp startled Cerridwen out of her moment of hope. Her attention shot up to the villager standing at the entrance to the tent. She dropped the small wooden box she was holding, and it clattered on the ground. Cerridwen winced slightly at the loud sound, hoping no one else had heard it. Fortunately, everyone else seemed distracted by the young woman and her guide conversing with the village leader. Cerridwen heaved a sigh of relief. The village woman held Cerridwen's gaze.

"Who...what are you?" she asked, her voice more curious than fearful.

I am no one of importance to you.

"You seem rather—attached to that ring. You know it no longer works, right? She gave it to me, hoping I could fix it. But even I am unsure that I can," she replied calmly.

Perhaps I can fix it, but not here.

"Why would you care? It's just a ring with magic."

It is far more than just simple magic, believe me. It never belonged in this galaxy; it will be of far more use at its original home if you allow me to take care of it.

"What will I tell *her*?" the villager asked, gesturing toward the main tent.

Whatever you would like. She will probably not believe you anyway.

This woman was no longer a threat, so Cerridwen turned away and started her ascent to the skies. The woman stopped her before she got too far.

"It isn't a ring, is it?"

Cerridwen swirled around and looked down at the woman with intrigue, *no, it is not.*

"Did it really even help her?"

Cerridwen looked back at the tent and saw the young woman emerge with her guide. She stared at her for some time before replying to the woman, *No, I do not believe she even needed its power. She is strong on her own; the sooner she sees that the sooner she can reach her full potential.*

Cerridwen floated high into the sky, leaving the villager in awe at her words. As the goddess flew high above the land, she held the ring tightly and whispered the phrase *tilleadh*. Suddenly, she felt herself being tugged out of the solar system. Planets flew by her in hyper speed as familiar constellations came into view. The familiar horizon of Morrighan's planet came into view as she felt her projection again meet with her body. The world turned dark again for a split second, but she regained consciousness quickly—the ring remained with her.

Morrighan and Arwn released their grip on her as Cerridwen presented to Morrighan the ring containing her love's soul. Morrighan took the ring ever so carefully. Her bottom lip trembled, and her voice quivered, "Macha ...can you hear me?"

Yes! The voice resounded with excitement. It was the loudest Cerridwen had ever heard it.

"We will bring you back, My Love!" Morrighan vowed.

"Wait, you said nothing about bringing her back. I thought we were just going to ask her about the Dullahan," said Cerridwen.

"She can barely say anything in this state. If you want your answers, we must bring her back," Morrighan insisted.

"And what would that entail?" Cerridwen asked through gritted teeth.

Morrighan placed the ring carefully on the ground in the center of the three. She stood back up and looked at Cerridwen with a devious smile, "Why, I'm glad you asked."

Without hesitation, Morrighan reached out for Cerridwen's hand. She conjured a sharp blade and sliced her hand, squeezing the blood onto the ring. Cerridwen cried out in pain as she ripped her hand away, nursing her injury. She looked at Morrighan in horror, who moved on to her own hand as Arwn sliced his hand as well. As their blood dropped onto the ring, covering the piece of jewelry, Morrighan began chanting another celestial chant, one Cerridwen knew for certain was a creation of her own. But it seemed to work. The ground beneath the ring started to quake as the ring began to glow. It levitated in the air and the blood which had pooled around the ring began to form a shape with it.

Cerridwen backed up in horror as the ring hovered in the center while the blood formed a chest and neck. While the blood engulfed the ring and finished off with the head. Morrighan's chanting ceased while she shifted to a new incantation with which Cerridwen was familiar. The dirt around them departed from the ground and started to cling to this new form, hardening like armor. Soon, jet-black eyes snapped open, and thin, pale lips curved into a wicked smile. Wild black flowing hair cascaded down her back in perfect waves. Macha was reborn.

Tears began to drip down Morrighan's face as she approached Macha. She, in turn, replied with a joyous smile—well, that's how Cerridwen interpreted it anyway. The two lovers embraced and finally reunited.

Cerridwen had never seen this type of relationship between two dark entities—pure love. But this was such a small victory. Hesitantly, she cleared her throat, "Um, I'm sorry to interrupt this union, but we...we still need some answers about the Dullahan."

Macha stepped back from Morrighan and faced Cerridwen, "You saved me when no one else could or, in some cases, would. Thank you, Cerridwen. I am in your debt. I will answer any question you have about him if it is within my power."

Cerridwen didn't waste any time, "What is his weakness. He must have one."

Macha seemed to be unsettled by this question. Morrighan held her hand and wrapped an arm around her in comfort. Macha let out a soft, gurgled sigh as she replied, "He does, but I am unsure how we can use it."

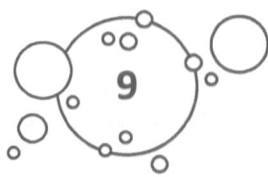

9

Vincent's world shook, and his eyes fluttered open. He had dozed off in a chair by the pond and couldn't quite remember what he had dreamed of, but he was sure it was one he had many times. He rubbed the sleep from his eyes and brushed a hand through his tousled hair. He looked around to see what had broken him from his afternoon nap and saw Benji hovering over him. But it wasn't Benji who wanted his attention—he was just the messenger.

Benji turned his focus off in the distance, which drew Vincent's gaze. Markus ran down the small incline toward them as fast as his legs could carry him—panic etched into his normally calm face. Vincent slowly rose from his position and took in the rest of his surroundings. No one else seemed to be present. Avelia had already left just as he was about to fall asleep, and he couldn't see Conall's car anywhere, so he must have gone to pout elsewhere. That's all he seemed to do these days. All seemed to be very quiet—the calm before the storm.

"Siochain, what is it?" Benji asked as Markus finally reached them.

Markus suddenly stopped, "It's...it's Moira. She will not wake up."

"Perhaps she and Saol had an eventful night," Vincent said with a slight smirk.

"Very mature, Brother." Markus rolled his eyes, "It just so happens that he cannot revive her either. She is alive, but barely."

"Could one of the children's spells have gone awry?" asked Benji, showing a little concern.

"No, they have been with Merlin, but I think you might be on to something," Markus said, glancing back at the castle, "Her entire body is engulfed in a rather strange glow, something I had never seen. She is not in pain but sleeping peacefully, and according to Saol, she is not ill."

Of Markus' entire comment, Vincent only caught one word—glow. He furrowed his eyebrows in concentration. He knew Moira had a type of magic unfamiliar to the rest of the Avalonians, but she wasn't experienced enough to attempt a spell. Even an incantation of her own wouldn't result in this. Suddenly, flashes of his dream swelled to the surface of his thoughts. He quickly interrupted Markus, who was rambling on about possible theories, "What color was the glow around her?"

Markus shook his head, not following his train of thought, "A light purple—almost lavender in color. But I fail to see why that would explain anything."

Vincent was already bolting toward the castle at Markus' last few words. He couldn't be sure, but that description resembled what he continued to see in his dreams. It almost felt like an omen. As he raced down the hall, he could hear the hurried footsteps of his brothers trailing behind him. He rounded the corner and burst through the door of Arthur and Moira's room to see clothes and books scattered everywhere. He turned his head toward the bed to see Arthur kneeling beside it, holding Moira's hand. He had a faint magical glow emanating from his other hand, possibly a final attempt at reviving her. He hadn't changed out of his evening clothes. He was probably trying to figure out the cause of her condition, which would explain the books everywhere. As for the clothing, perhaps his theory of an eventful night wasn't too far off.

Vincent stepped further into the room as Markus and Benji finally caught up to him. All three stared at Moira's still figure engulfed in that strange glow. Arthur finally rested his hand, and his magical glow faded—he looked defeated.

"I have tried every spell that I know. Nothing seems to have any effect," he said solemnly.

"Could this have something to do with her anti-magic abilities—you know, the ones that allowed her to see us as we are?" asked Benji.

Arthur shook his head, "I had initially considered that, and if that were so, there would be nothing anyone could do, not even Merlin with all his relics."

Arthur looked at his brothers, and his attention quickly shot toward Vincent, who remained strangely quiet—staring at Moira. He slowly rose to his feet, keeping his eyes fixed on Vincent.

"You know something, don't you, Taghd," he said cautiously.

A bead of sweat escaped Vincent's forehead and sneaked down the side of his face—his dream was beginning to come back to him, one that he now realized he had had many times before. *It can't be. What does telling them do? It will only cause conflict among us, which we do not need.*

"You say she has been like this since you woke this morning?" asked Vincent, ignoring Arthur's question.

"Yes, I'll ask you again, what do you know?"

Vincent turned toward the door, trying to avoid the situation, but Arthur wouldn't let this go. He reached out toward Vincent and grabbed his wrist, yanking him back. Suddenly, the periwinkle glow from Moira extended out like tendrils, each tendril wrapping around the brothers, paralyzing them before dragging them into the same deep slumber as Moira.

Darkness surrounded Vincent, a darkness he had never experienced, even in his world. He turned every which way, but he couldn't locate the others. Panic set in when suddenly a familiar, disembodied voice echoed all around.

"Remember who ye are!"

Moira, either she created this spell or something more powerful than her is controlling this. A bright light shone in the corner where Arthur was illuminated, followed shortly by Markus, Benji, and finally Vincent. He covered his eyes, hoping to glean more information about this strange dark abyss.

"Moira, what is this place," Arthur's voice echoed.

"Remember who ye are!" she repeated.

Vincent felt his body lurch forward. From a quick glance, the others were forced to do the same. He looked straight ahead to where the magic was taking them as a portal slowly began to form—a portal that revealed his darkest dreams.

***

Vincent's eyes fluttered open. He looked up at the crudely built stone ceiling and smiled. He had another pleasant evening. He slowly rose from his fur-lined bed to see three young women lying around him, their bodies barely covered with the remaining fur blankets—all fast asleep, also pleased with the previous evening. A loud shriek broke his peaceful revere and echoed off the walls of his large room. His eyes rolled as the women around him began to stir. *Not again.* Was all he could think. With a wave of his hand, the women around him disappeared as if they had never even existed, perhaps they did only in his magical mind.

The god casually jumped out of his four-poster bed and walked over to the massive fireplace where a fire continued to roar—that was the one thing he liked about this world he called a prison—nothing truly died, not unless he and his brothers wanted it to. Speaking of brothers, that type of scream could have only come from one of them. Vincent heaved a heavy sigh as he conjured himself a wardrobe to cover his naked body before exiting his room.

The dark hallways were filled with strange noises with every step he took. Dark violet veins pulsated at different speeds, reminding Vincent that the planet formed around him, adding to the prison world concept. Although, he and his brothers were free to move around from this planet to others, provided they were doing work for their Creator. He passed another partially open room; inside, he saw Markus pouring over a large war table. He always created strategies for collecting subjects for the Creator's experience. It was during these times he learned not to disturb the process. Benji turned the corner of the table and waved a hand over it. Elements on the table rose, adding more to Markus' plan. Benji spoke quietly, and Markus nodded in agreement, still contemplating his initial plan. Benji rarely spent time alone unless it was to create another spell to inflict a new illness on the Creator's subjects.

As he passed the door, the hallway turned a sharp corner. Another scream pierced the air, originating from a door in the shadows. Arthur emerged from the room, wiping his bloody hands on a dirty rag nonchalantly. A chill shot up Vincent's spine. Of all his brothers—Arthur was the one he feared the most. Arthur looked up at Vincent and smirked, gesturing back to the room. "I wouldn't go in there; not much left."

His callous tone made Vincent even more anxious. No one spoke to him to ask if they could help with it. He spent most of his time conducting terrible experiments—on the dead. The Creator seemed to always favor Arthur, probably due to his indifference about which creature he experimented on. He was never particular about what creature he used, whether it was a dead animal or human that was considered lost on Avalon. To him, no one would necessarily miss them. He never killed anything, but the experiments he conducted were atrocious. The Creator insisted on learning about the weaknesses of others, and Arthur never questioned why. He was the closest to the Creator, and although he never showed emotions, he rarely berated him, which was as close to compassion as they could ever get.

Arthur shoved the rag into his back pocket and walked over to Vincent, putting an arm around him, "Come, Brother, *he* wants to see us.

The only other thing that ever struck fear in Vincent was an impromptu meeting with the Creator. He expressed no emotion at Arthur's words in fear of retribution. He nodded and allowed Arthur to guide him to the Creator's lair. With every step he took, he felt more and more dread sinking in. When they finally reached the Creator, he was standing in the center of a circular room, looking at a holographic map of the galaxy. Vincent could see the small trace of their planet with at least six other planets around them. Vincent discreetly rolled his eyes. That's all the Creator would do, stare at this map, day in and day out, as if it would change anything. Of course, he never spoke to them about his true plans. In Vincent's mind, having all the information would help him more. But he figured there was a reason the

Creator wasn't being entirely honest—he was hiding something.

The headless figure didn't turn toward the brothers as they entered but rather continued to lift his decapitated head toward different areas of the map, "Did your experiment work, Saol?"

"Negative. Despite it being a corpse, it was a little too—*animated*. I had to destroy it again," Arthur replied, sounding more annoyed.

The Creator shrugged as if Arthur's attempt had little consequence: "Try again."

Arthur flinched at the carelessness in the Creator's tone, "I have tried, many times—endlessly. I need something different. These Avalonians and other creatures have similar compositions."

"The subjects I have given you are not agreeable?" the Creator asked, slowly turning around.

Vincent stepped away from Arthur, knowing what would occur next. Arthur glanced nervously from Vincent to the Creator; he swallowed the fear rising in his throat, "No, they are agreeable. We...we might find a different outcome were we to get different subjects."

The Creator was now mere inches from Arthur. He raised his head and stared at him; his face was expressionless, which added more to the fear that resonated within both brothers. Without shifting his gaze, the Creator directed his next question to Vincent, "What are your thoughts, Taghd. I am certain you have opinions on the matter?"

Vincent stuttered a bit, completely taken off guard with the question, "Uh, I would give my opinion if I knew why Saol was experimenting on these—creatures."

The Creator's gaze shifted momentarily to Vincent, who started wishing he hadn't said anything. Approaching footsteps alerted them all to the arrival of Markus and Benji, who, judging by their expressions, seemed to bear good news. This was a welcome distraction to Vincent and Arthur as the Creator returned to his map, where the other brothers met with him.

"What news do you bring?" asked the Creator.

Markus glanced around the room as if trying to keep something quiet, "Well, um, it could work. But we would need far more power than we currently have."

The Creator stared into the holographic map and said, "More power will not delay our plan. Coimhlint, are you prepared for the next phase of the experiment?"

Benji shifted uncomfortably, though he tried to hide it as best he could, "Yes, if we can secure more subjects, I see no reason why it wouldn't work."

"Then consider this mission a success. I will secure the power, and you four prepare yourselves for the next phase. I will call on you when I am ready."

Markus and Benji were quick to leave, followed shortly by Arthur, who muttered obscenities under his breath as he left, angry about how his meeting with the Creator had gone. Conversely, Vincent remained the longest; he stared at the Creator with confusion and fear. Something was terribly wrong. He seemed to only tell the four of them parts of his plan. He knew the brothers would be on his side, regardless of the plan, and that's how the Creator made them devoted servants to him. There must have been something he knew they would never agree to—something Vincent was determined to find out.

"Is there something I can assist you with, Taghd?"

Vincent saw the Creator had turned his head completely around. His piercing eyes seemed to bore into Vincent's soul. The young god simply shook his head no and turned toward the exit. He could still feel the Creator's eyes on him as he left.

***

"You are being paranoid, Brother," said Markus, stuffing a strange fruit into his mouth.

The gods had gathered around a large table where a feast had been laid out for them. This was their typical meeting place. They didn't need to consume food to survive. It was merely a pass time for them to discuss what experiments they'd been working on. But tonight was different. There was no talk of experiments or even magic. Vincent's words consumed their thoughts.

"I am not. He's been acting different. You can't tell me that you haven't noticed. He only tells us part of his plans these days. Something must seem strange about that," said Vincent.

"He knows we speak with each other during times like this. Perhaps he feels repeating himself is a waste of his time," said Benji.

"Well then, what has he told all of you?" Vincent challenged.

Arthur spoke first, "He wants to see the subject's weakness. That is why he has me testing my *skills* on whatever and whoever we can find. The humans and creatures on the planet Avalon are not exactly being sought after. They were only ever deceased, to begin with. No harm there. But when I resurrect them, they are but husks. No thought, no emotion...just a soulless vessel."

Markus and Benji weren't as forthcoming about their projects. They couldn't exactly look Vincent in the eye, either. Vincent didn't take his eyes off them for a second, "Your turn."

Markus sighed, trying to find a clever way of not revealing everything. However, he knew Vincent would read between the lines no matter what he said, "Fine, he has given me a map of another galaxy—several galaxies, in fact, that all contain other humans not created on Avalon, a place called Earth, well multiple versions of Earth that is. We know nothing about the planet except that there are more humans than Avalon a thousand times over. He wants them, but he does not have the power to reach that world regardless of the dimension. That's something which has bothered him for—a long time."

Benji rolled his eyes, piggybacking off of Markus' comment, "And I can only assume that his desires for the humans of this Earth planet fall on me. He has me working with Markus to see how we can create diversions of illnesses to bring humans to our planet for such experiments. He has never divulged his reasons for wanting these specific humans."

"What about you, Taghd? You seem to be the one running this little meeting, yet you have not mentioned your role in all of this," Arthur said accusatory.

"I have none," he replied, embarrassed, "He has never given me instructions. He allows me to do what I would like."

"Well, aren't you fortunate," Benji replied sarcastically.

"Not exactly. He favors you three. I'm just an accident that is of no use to him."

Markus shook his head, "I'm sure he does not see you like that. You are of help!"

"I have fictitious humans in my bed every night, and we partake in activities that cause hallucinogens. How does that help the Creator?"

The other three exchanged uncertain glances. Benji shrugged, "Perhaps you are his experiment, seeing how humans react to this type of attention?"

Vincent drained his wine goblet and rose from the table, "Thank you for the boost of confidence, but let's not fool ourselves."

He could hear the others conversing with each other as he left the room, all perhaps trying to find a way to remedy his depressed mind. But nothing would resolve this. He was determined in his opinions about what the Creator was up to and where he stood with him.

Later that evening, Vincent found himself lying down in bed alone. He didn't want the company of others or the assistance of his hallucinogens. He just wanted to be alone, but he was also bored, and when he was bored, he often found himself getting into trouble. He stared up at the ceiling, and with a wave of his hand, a holographic screen appeared. Across the screen came images of his brothers going about the missions the Creator gave them—some struggling in vain. Suddenly, the image seemed to glitch, and a lavender-colored energy force covered the screen, shifting the images to the Creator, who did not want to be seen.

Vincent sat up in bed, peering closer to the image—an image he knew he wasn't supposed to see. The Creator was exiting from a room that Vincent had never seen, and he spent most of his time exploring the planet. This room appeared hidden within the Creator's inner lair, where none of the gods were allowed to go. Vincent zoomed in on the image, trying to get a better look at the small, hidden room, but nothing was aglow. Nothing magical appeared to make this room any more special than the others—it looked normal. But something inside the Creator did *not* want the others to find. That's where Vincent was certain he'd start looking for some answers. But how to get there without the Creator knowing? He knew everything and was seemingly everywhere.

As if hearing his thoughts, the lavender-colored magic shot its way toward Vincent and sucked him into the image. Within seconds, he found himself on the floor of the Creator's inner lair. He quickly looked around to ensure his arrival didn't cause a stir, but with the Creator nowhere to be seen, Vincent had to wonder if that image he had just seen was a live projection. He looked around the room to see a table with what appeared to be failed chemical experiments, some of which still exhausted strange odors. No bed could be seen in this room, but the Creator hardly ever slept. He needed sleep and sustenance less than his offspring.

Vincent looked off to the corner to see where the hidden room was. As he approached, the wall began to split in half, revealing a small room. He looked around, ensuring he was alone, and cautiously walked in. Upon first glance, the room was much smaller than he expected, and it was fairly empty except for the few jars of unidentifiable objects lining the walls. A small wooden table stood in the center, its surface stained with dark red blood. Vincent shirks away from it, not wanting to think what terrible acts were committed in this room, but he didn't have to think about it for long. As he glanced closer at the elements in the room, that strange glow returned, jumping between the jars on the wall. He followed the bouncing ball of energy as it hopped around the room.

"What are you? What are you trying to show me?" Vincent whispered, trying to follow the magic.

Suddenly, it stopped at a jar that seemed to be a deformed heart of sorts upon closer examination. Vincent felt strangely drawn to the heart, as if he almost knew who it belonged to. He touched the cold glass with the tip of his finger, and a vision suddenly appeared. Flashes of blood and limbs crossed his mind so fast it jolted him backward into the blood-stained table. His heart raced as he digested just exactly what he saw.

"No, that that's impossible," Vincent exclaimed, fear-stricken.

"What are you doing in here?"

Vincent turned toward the entrance to see Arthur stepping in. He looked around, also seeming to be unfamiliar with this room. But it doesn't seem to faze him, considering the experiments he typically works on.

"You know of this place?" asked Vincent, regaining his composure.

"No, but it does not surprise me. The Creator must have his secrets too, I suppose," Arthur replied as he examined jarred intestines, "But what really intrigues me is that strange purple light I keep seeing around the planet."

"You see it too? I thought it was just calling out to me!" Vincent said as he looked for the foreign magic.

"I've only seen it from a distance, but be happy the Creator hasn't seen it. I don't think they are friends."

"They?"

Arthur shook his head, "It comes from a far more powerful source. I assume it belongs to an entity. It seems to always disappear whenever the Creator is around. At least from what I've noticed."

"I can understand why," Vincent replied, looking back at the heart.

"What did you see?"

Vincent silently gestured for Arthur to take a look, too. He could only hope that the magic was still in effect. Arthur touched the glass and his eyes widened in fear, or the closest comparison to fear. He stepped back slowly and looked at the other jars, including the table behind him. He looked at Vincent and quietly said, "We have to tell the others."

"Would they believe us?"

"I'm not sure. I don't even believe we'd be able to show them. It's not like we can bring them here without the Creator getting suspicious," said Vincent.

"He probably already is. The fact that he has not found us definitely indicates something is wrong."

"Come, let's find Siochain and Coimhlint. Whether they believe us or not, we still need to tell them," Vincent replied, starting toward the door and leaving the room of horror behind.

***

Benji waved his hands in disagreement at Vincent, "That is the most absurd thing I have ever heard."

"I agree. What proof do you have?" Markus chimed in.

Vincent and Arthur had summoned the others to a meeting at the feast table. But this time, the massive table was barren, and no one sat down and relaxed. Benji had been pacing since Vincent gave the announcement of the vision. Markus sat down with his head in his hands, and Vincent and Arthur both stood by their chairs, ready to leave or change topics should the Creator interrupt their meeting.

"We do," said Vincent for what felt like the fifth time.

"Yes, you've already mentioned a small closet inside the Creator's inner lair, which you have yet to explain how you initially arrived," said Benji.

"What part of foreign magic did you not understand?"

"Yes, you made that quite clear, but a magic that the Creator doesn't control. Don't you find that rather odd? Perhaps this is one of his tests?" suggested Markus.

"No, he wouldn't compromise himself like that. This was another magic," Vincent assured.

"I'm sorry, but if you have no proof, then—" started Benji.

A thunderous sound roared around them as that familiar lavender-colored magic soared around them, striking the walls with lightning. The gods ducked as fragments of the walls and ceiling started falling all around. As more sparks of lighting emerged from all around, the bolts converged onto one section of the wall, slowly forming into an energized portal that revealed the same images that Vincent and Arthur had once witnessed. But this time, all of them saw this vision in its entirety.

The image started with the Creator speaking with a feminine looking creature whose composition was mainly of blood. She appeared drawn to him—almost mesmerized. The Creator, however, didn't seem remotely interested in her the same way. But he did capitalize on her emotional state. The next scene showed something far more grotesque, and some of the gods had to even look away. But Vincent couldn't take his eyes off the horror. The Creator ripped the blood creature's soul from her body. It crystallized into a small shape the size of a stone. The soul throbbed a crimson color as he held it. He shrugged, not seeing the need anymore, and magically threw it far out of the solar system. Shortly after, he began ripping her body apart, limb from limb. Her internal organs he jarred and carefully placed on a shelf. As for what he did with her body parts, that was an entirely different horror story. The next scene showed him piecing together four creations, each containing part of the former blood creature. The Creator nodded contentedly with his design. Satisfied he used all the pieces he needed, the Creator stretched out his hands over the four bodies, and a violet crystallized stream of magic pooled over the bodies, conforming to the existing limbs filling in the missing pieces of the bodies.

All four gods inched closer to the vision screen, all standing in a row next to each other—their eyes glued to the next part in horror. The screen revealed the full completion of these monsters—they were them. Slowly, one by one, the gods on the screen opened their eyes, unaware of how they were created until now.

The vision ended, leaving the gods confused and conflicted. They all looked down at their limbs, feeling like they were having an out-of-body experience. Markus, however, was the first to break from the revere.

"This is madness, so what if he used a blood creature to make us. We're magical beings."

"You cannot mean that. The creature seemed to adore the Creator. I don't believe she would be willing to give her life away like that," said Vincent.

"Well, at the very least, we know he lied to us," said Arthur, "He said we were born from the stars, a gift from the heavens to assist him in his work."

"And yet, we don't exactly know why he wants us to work towards the Earth goal. Perhaps we are being fooled and should consider deciding for ourselves what *we* would like to do," suggested Benji, starting to get on board with Vincent and Arthur.

"Free will. That was an error in your programming," came a haunting voice.

The Creator had secretly entered the room at some point in their observation of the vision. As usual, his facial expression hadn't changed. It was as monotone as his tone. This always made it difficult for the gods to decide how to communicate with him. With a snap of his fingers, he walked around the table and made it disappear, followed by the chairs. Simultaneously, the gods backed away from their master, terrified of what he'd do next—even that was sometimes difficult to predict.

"Why were we created?" Vincent challenged the Creator, his mind and body in full adrenaline.

"To assist me," replied the Creator simply.

He was beginning to respond with as few words as possible. Vincent knew what that meant...he was getting angry.

The gods exchanged knowing looks. They, too, knew what this meant. They began to tread cautiously with their line of questioning. Benji piped up next, "Why are you interested in the humans of the planet Earth?"

"They have something that I require," he replied matter-of-factly.

"And your collection of organs can help you obtain that?" asked Markus, trying to get more information from the Creator.

"The organs of a goddess are valuable in experiments."

"Might we circle back to the human experimentation? What kind of people on Earth are you planning to use?" asked Arthur.

"Does that matter? They are all made of the same composition."

The gods looked at each other, all feeling rather uncomfortable with his words. Arthur looked down at the ground, "You are not considering just the deceased? That's all I've ever worked on."

"And wouldn't living humans be more obvious if they went missing?" Markus chimed in.

"That matters not when we take over all the Earths," said the Creator, his mouth curving into a slight smile.

The gods stared at him, terrified. That was the first sign of emotion he ever revealed. Vincent felt anger well within him, "Occasional experimentation and a fun night is one thing, but taking over planets. That's going too far. What if, in your endeavors, you destroy all those worlds?"

"We have a plan."

"I'm sorry, *we*? Who else are you working with—or for?" Benji asked, growing angry.

"You are all too clever. Another failure in your creation," the Creator replied, his hand reaching for his magical dagger dangling from his waist.

The gods were charging up their magic and reaching for their weapons when Vincent replied, "Good, you can admit to your mistakes. Perhaps you have some humanity in you after all."

A clash of metal and bursts of magic filled the air as the brothers flew at their Creator—each blow failing miserably. The Creator attached his head to the belt on his side and began using both hands to attack at different angles. Vincent slowed down momentarily, trying to catch his breath. None of their magic was working on their Creator. To him, it made sense; why make a creation that could theoretically turn on you? But the brothers' occasional strike with weapons seemed to have a marginal effect. Benji started reaching for another weapon he had hidden in his pant leg when suddenly the Creator took a sharp left and started toward Vincent, who was unprepared for an attack. Benji suddenly bolted between Vincent and the Creator, lunging his hand toward the Creator to stop him. His hand unexpectedly plunged into the Creator's chest. Benji could feel his master weakening and in surprised pain. He knew what he had to do to stop this fight. He grabbed at a bone and, with ease, ripped it from the Creator. The monster fell back in pain as the force of the battle equally flew Benji backward. He looked at his bloody hand to see that the bone was forming into the shape of a dagger. Quickly, he sheathed it in the band of his pants as he started to get up.

As the Creator writhed in pain, the gods stared at him in awe. An unexpected golden glow started to swirl around them, making them slowly disappear. Within seconds, they were on an entirely different planet that they had never seen before. But that wasn't their biggest concern, but rather the origin of their rescue. A golden goddess stood regally before them, entirely unfazed by their disheveled appearance. The golden glow rescinded back to her side, where she placed her hands daintily in front of her.

"You did well," the goddess congratulated with a smile.

Vincent allowed his eyes to adjust to the light of this new planet. It was dark in ambiance and consisted of a red-ish hue. The world around him smelled eerily like iron—blood if he had to guess. But there was no blood to be found, the planet lay barren like a wasteland. As if the deity who controlled it no longer resided there. *Macha, this must have been her world!*

As this thought crossed his mind, so did the memory of the spell he cast just before they vanished. Although he couldn't remember exactly what conversation took place, he knew that the woman before him was no friend. He looked over at his brothers, Arthur and Markus who simply looked at their strange new surroundings. Vincent then looked to Benji who looked confused at the bloody bone he ripped from their master in the previous battle. Benji looked back up at the goddess and in a fit of anger and fear threw the sharp object at her.

The goddess quickly halted the speed of the weapon and with a wave of her hand opened a portal, sending the bone away.

"I do not think that weapons will be necessary, after all, I am unarmed and only wish to help you!"

For a moment, Vincent almost regretted protecting just himself with the spell. But given Benji's violent reactionary tendencies, Vincent could now see it was for the best. He put on the best confused expression that he could muster, playing into whatever plan the goddess had conjured.

"Who...who are you?" asked Vincent.

"I am Danu, the Mother Goddess to the other planets you see," she replied, gesturing to the sky, "I rescued you from a very dangerous situation, and I wish to give you an offer."

The brothers exchanged uncertain looks. They found this particular creature to be just as unsettling as their Creator.

"I...I don't recall where we were that required a rescue," said Arthur suspiciously.

"Oh, you needn't worry about the danger, you are all perfectly fine here. And will forever be safe," Danu

"Why would you care about us?" Benji challenged.

Danu sized the gods up and chuckled slightly, "I do not think that *care* is the correct word in this situation. Perhaps an investment is the better term. You four are powerful deities, as I am certain you can feel a power surge through your very veins. In fact, I believe you can grow to protect this solar system."

"What does it need protecting from?" asked Vincent, hoping his prodding didn't give too much away.

Danu wasn't prepared for the brothers to pelt her with questions. She inhaled deeply and gave him a sweetly sick smile, "This plant you stand on is the link that binds all of the other planets in this solar system together. You four will take a portion of the planet and create your own kingdom and you must only stay within your realm, with the exception of a unified meeting space to discuss your realm's contribution to the protection."

"What kind of power do we possess?" asked Markus.

Danu was struggling, she stuttered ever so slightly before cleverly saying, "That, My Dear, is something you shall have to figure out in the realm of your choosing. This planet will...grant you knowledge of your power."

Vincent was impressed with her quick thinking. If he wasn't of clear mind, even he'd have bought her lies. But how long could she keep it up for? Especially if she were to leave them there alone.

"I shall be watching all of you, I believe you will make this solar system proud and you will do fine!" said Danu.

And there it is. We are in solitary confinement until she has no use for us. Can I hide the truth for that long?

Vincent, Arthur, Markus, and Benji watched as the creature before them disappeared into a golden light, vanishing from their new world. Immediately they felt their bodies being pulled in the opposite direction from each other. All four being led to their new and uncertain life.

***

Vincent's mind returned to the black abyss. He looked at his brothers, who were still illuminated by the magical spotlight. They all looked confused and conflicted. Only Vincent was able to keep this secret for so long—the secret that haunted his dreams every night. Benji looked at Vincent, the only one who didn't look horrified, "You knew this entire time? Why didn't you tell us?"

"We were being watched and she didn't know that I knew. Besides, I didn't know what plan she actually had for us, other than to leave us for eternity. I was tired of being a servant to that monster. Living on our former *mother's* planet seemed like a better alternative. Besides, I wasn't lying—I was having fun on that planet.," he replied plainly.

Markus chimed in and shook his head, "Taghd has a point. There's nothing he could have done."

"We wouldn't have known too!" said Benji.

"And watch you explode like you typically do at any bad news?" asked Vincent sarcastically, "I'm sorry, Brother, but your talents do not lie in the arts of acting."

Arthur quickly changed the topic, addressing Moira, "What does this solve anyway?"

"Remember who ye are!" Moira's disembodied voice echoed again.

"We do remember. What more is there?"

"Choose!" she replied swiftly.

"Moira, we don't understand. What are we choosing?" asked Arthur gently.

A wind picked up around them, and the voice replied, "Yerselves. Choose the past and forget the present, or choose the present and forever forget the past."

"Is there option c?" asked Vincent, noticing nothing around them had changed.

The wind continued to blow, waiting for an answer. One verbal decision was all it required. Vincent watched as his brothers contemplated this decision. Arthur wouldn't agree with the past; he was far too in love with Moira. Markus seemed to enjoy his peaceful existence, and Benji—well, Benji was changing for the good. He'd hate to have forgotten all of this adventure. As for Vincent, he always knew nothing changed for him. But to him, there was more of a consequence behind her words. They were powerful before they changed, but they also matured and learned about themselves. Wouldn't the knowledge of the present be even more powerful than the strength of their past? He wasn't the only one contemplating this as Arthur spoke up, surprising him.

"Accept the past for what it is and embrace the future for what it could be."

He said it in such a hushed tone Vincent almost didn't hear him until he repeated it one more time, but louder and toward the sky.

"Accept the past for what it is and embrace the future for what it could be. We...we choose both!"

The bright lights around them grew brighter until it nearly blinded them, causing them to shield their eyes. It rapidly died down, and the brothers were returned to Arthur's bedroom. The only difference now is that Moira was no longer there. Benji looked out the window and said, "You must be joking." He bolted out the door, with the others following close behind. As they ran onto the castle grounds, they met Moira, who appeared as if nothing had happened.

"What...what was all of that about?" asked Arthur, nearly out of breath.

"I agree, that was a bit unnecessary, don't you think?" asked Benji.

Moira simply smiled at all of them. She slightly chuckled, "No, ah, don't think so. Arthur was right; ya needed both the past and the present, and for that, you have all yer memories restored and all of yer powers—plus some."

Vincent could feel something was different the second they returned. But he didn't know what, and now wasn't the time to figure that out. A loud, thunderous roar echoed around them, shaking the ground. Even Moira looked rattled by the sudden interruption. Vincent furrowed his brow. He knew what this meant—war was coming.

10

Clarity, tranquility, acceptance. These concepts rang throughout Moria's peaceful mind like a harmonic symphony—feelings she had never dared to dream of. But the strange world around her reflected the opposite. A cacophony of screams, shrieks, and roars of the enemy began to drown out her peaceful mind. She gathered her strength, which seemed to return in waves of power, and rose to her feet. Her thin brows furrowed as her eyes darted all around, trying to identify which planet they were on. But it wasn't just any planet, but fractions of them all. She stood in this dome with kaleidoscope walls, all revealing some aspect of all the planets. The walls were created by a strange violet crystal that could only come from one creature—the Dullahan.

As if on cue, the monster materialized before her. It was at this moment she realized she wasn't alone. Arthur and his brothers stood in a group nearest her while Merlin and the children stood a ways off in the distance. Conall stood by himself, but he looked rather unwell since the last time Moira saw him. Perhaps war didn't agree with him as it did with his ancestors. *How would ah know that?* Moira thought. Then again, she was different now.

Nearest to her stood Morrighan, Arwen, and Macha, and although Cerridwen was nowhere to be seen, a faint glow encompassed the three as if in a protective shield. None of the gods and Avalonians took their eyes off the Dullahan, who seemed to tower over them all. He stood in the center of the dome with his head at his side and his other hand caressing the pummel of a large, black blade that looked lethal with just the touch.

As usual, his decapitated head revealed no emotion, and his posture gave no indication as to what he was about to do next. He waved his hand off to the side, and Danu appeared, violet crystallized bindings wrapped tightly around her—

squeezing the life out of her, but she still remained undefeated.

Arthur spoke up, and Moira could hear his voice softly echoing in her ear. "Did he bring her as a bargaining chip? She is no friend to us."

Benji seemed to agree with one caveat, "True, but I think I speak for everyone when I say that he's higher on our kill list."

Moira pondered on both statements; both were right, and the Dullahan knew that. So why reveal her imprisonment? She felt confused, but there it was again, that unfamiliar clarity. She knew exactly why he was doing it—to incite a reaction. She shook her head, and the Dullahan took notice.

"I am not your nemesis. I have done nothing to you but give you a new purpose of living. Danu, in her vanity, wanted to control you. Now is your opportunity to enact your vengeance."

He wasn't exactly wrong. That's what made this all worse. Killing Danu felt pretty low on his priority list for Moira. *Ye can end this. It doesn't have to drag out.* The voice was hers, but that wasn't what she was thinking at that moment. It was the other part of her—the new part that was trying to break through. She tried tapping into that peace she felt moments ago, but it was drowned out by another voice.

"She will pay for her crimes against us, but on our terms. We do not need your permission," spat Conall weakly.

No, stop speaking! That is what he wants. Don't engage him! The voice came again, but it was louder. *Ye need to speak up. Let us do our job. Let us do what we were born to do!*

Moira rolled her eyes at the inner thought, but something quickly caught her eye. The Dullahan looked at Conall, no emotion whatsoever, but something sped behind his eyes— like code to a computer program. But this was unlike any programming she had ever seen. The code soon disappeared, leaving his usual creepy eyes. The Dullahan shrugged his shoulders and snapped Danu away; his initial plan failed. It was time to change tactics.

"You wish to end my existence. Your magic has shifted, yet you are all unprepared."

The Dullahan said this so matter-of-fact that any reasonable person would want to encourage him to speak more and gather more information. But Macha, being the hothead that she was, lunged at the monster first, instigating the inevitable fight. Moira could hear the faint warning cry from Morrighan, calling her lover back. But Macha was out for blood. She raised her hand mid-air, and a dagger glinted in the light. The Dullahan didn't even turn his head when he withdrew his whip, wrapping it around her wrist and throwing Macha to the ground, instantly unconscious from the force. Moira saw it again in his eyes—that code. *Who are ye working for?* She wondered.

With Macha down for the count, the remaining heroes dove into the battle. The children were the most obvious with their new gifts. The two younger boys worked in tandem with a sword and shield. At the same time, the eldest focused his gaze on the Dullahan, a laser protruding which did very little to affect the monster. Skylar flew around him like an annoying fly, trying to scream her banshee cry, but it was drowned out by the humming of the crystallized creatures he had summoned, all of which started crawling out from the walls of the kaleidoscope. Although the children were a great distraction, they contributed little to the war effort, but their courage would be one for the history books.

Conall did something extraordinary, on the other hand, he transformed into a dragon Moira had never seen before. It almost appeared like a new breed. Its scales shimmered like diamonds, but its color was a bright orange. Its wings looked more like feathers, and its claws were like bird talons. This seemed to greatly affect the Dullahan as he, too did not expect this. Once again, his eyes became a computer. Conall flew around the Dullahan, the tips of his wings creating flames wherever they touched. While the Dullahan was distracted, Morrighan and Arwn pulled Macha off to the side, checking to see if she was still with the living. Satisfied she'd be okay; Morrighan drew out her swords and started for the Dullahan—Arwn on her heels with a flaming club.

The Dullahan's creatures started closing in around him, making it difficult for anyone to strike. Arthur stepped forward, he contorted his fingers toward the ground, and, one by one, moved them as if he were playing with a marionette. Corpses rose on his command—humans and animals. Some even emerging from the fractured worlds. The dead began fighting with the creatures, pulling them away from their master. He was truly the god of life and death. Markus dove into the fight, and although she met him as the god of peace, he was now also the god of war. Everywhere he stepped, he shifted the fighting as if he could control the emotions of the people around him. Benji and Markus remained somewhat the same since their transition, but to Moira, they had already chosen to be both past and future. Although, if she had to guess, they probably had some new tricks up their sleeve.

End this now! He already knows too much! Came the voice again.

"What can ah do? Everyone is already fighting, and ah can't even make a dent," said Moira to herself.

Ye know what to do, just like ye knew what to say to Arthur and his brothers. Stop thinking and just do it!

Moira drew in a deep breath and closed her eyes. Ignoring the battle cries around her, she voiced the feelings that had been struggling to the surface, "Clarity...tranquility...acceptance."

On that last word, she felt weightless, as if she were flying. In a way, she was, as her feet didn't touch the ground. She opened her eyes to see that the fighting had come to a slow motion. People seemed to float in midair—their poses ready to strike. She looked down at herself to see her body was covered in a periwinkle-colored gown that appeared to be made of air itself. Her long, bright red hair was a light pink with highlights that complimented her periwinkle dress. If she had to guess, her eyes had probably changed color as well. She drifted toward the Dullahan as the heroes around her slowly stopped their fighting and turned toward her. Even the Dullahan didn't expect this result. In fact, for the first time ever, he looked almost angry.

To her left, she could see Conall's dragon form was no longer distracted by her presence and he decided that her approaching the Dullahan was his cue to continue distracting him. But Moira, with the wave of her hand, froze the dragon in place, extinguishing the flaming tips of his wings. Although she appreciated his efforts, they were no longer necessary. With each step she took, the Dullahan grew more and more unstable, as if her very presence was toxic to him. Now, only a foot away, she stopped as he turned into his alien-like form, meeting her gaze.

"Ye will get no results from this squabble," her voice echoed loudly.

"I already have given all that I was instructed. Anything else was sent due to their actions," said the Dullahan, gesturing toward the frozen heroes.

"What do ye think this will accomplish, some data from a broken solar system?" she asked curiously.

"I am the messenger. I have no thought of my own," said the Dullahan. "There was no need to interfere. My true instructions were not to end them but to collect data. It appears that I have been compromised. The data they have received will have to suffice for now."

Moira opened her mouth to speak, but it was already too late. The Dullahan began to convulse and crumbled to the ground like a rag doll. Slowly, his form stopped moving, and seeing he was no longer a threat, Moira restored the world around her. The crystal creatures disappeared into thin air. Arthur retracted his army of the dead, returning them to their earthly homes. The dome fell in on itself as tiny pieces of space dust rained down on them, evaporating as it touched the ground. Moira waved her arms around her collecting the heroes in a magical grasp. The battle was won. It was time to go home.

***

Moira stared out over Camelot's grassy grounds as the world returned to as it was. Everyone was in a state of confusion but her. She knew exactly what happened but was unsure if the others were prepared for the answer. Conall was the first to approach her in his human form. He looked at her just as sickly as he had previously, but tears now streamed down his face.

"Please don't tell Avelia; she will want to fight my fate, and it's just not possible," he whispered to Moira, somehow knowing she already knew what he had become.

His words didn't catch Moira off guard at all. Conall made a deal with the dragon god, one that came at a hefty cost. He could not fight in the final battle as Avelia ordered, but there was a loophole to that magical command. If he tapped into his dragon magic and vowed to be the servant to the dragon god Sli, he would be transforming into a new creation. This would render his family's curse inert as he'd be tapping into another magic entirely. Alternatively, this would also mean he could never be with Avelia or his unborn child, as he'd have to be with the dragons, answering whatever task they needed of him. It might have seemed like an easy decision to make to help break a generational curse, but it would also mean he'd be living in a state of solitude. No one in his family dared to try this. Being in this new, upgraded form, he probably also has knowledge like the dragons—beyond his normal human self. He knew who and what she was.

"Ah will tell her ye died a hero," Moira replied solemnly.

"That—that would probably be best," he said, his eyes looking to the ground.

"Would someone mind telling me what just happened back there?" interrupted Benji, angry the fight was over before it really began.

Moira turned toward the confused gods and Avalonians, ready for an answer. She smiled at Conall, who stepped back, turning into his dragon form and disappearing into the sky.

"Moira?" Benji pressed, "You seem to be unusually calm. What happened?"

She sighed and braced herself for the inevitable arguments, "We were never in danger. The Dullahan was gathering information on us, as he has probably been doing for the last thousands of years. He wanted to see how we would react to his taunts and the environment, and we gave him exactly what he wanted. The Dullahan is a creation from another species in another time and another place. They are as old as time itself and, in their great power, will always be one step ahead of us."

After a brief moment of silence, Dakota spoke up, "Great pep talk. Got anything else, oh wise one?"

"He makes a valid point. How do you know all of this? What happened to you?" asked Macha.

Moira was relieved to see that Macha had returned to them, although, judging by her tone, she sounded more upset that she was out of the battle the moment it began.

"Ah am Moira as most of ye have already known me, but I am and have always been far more. From the moment ah was born, a magical spark ignited in me. All of ye have seen it in some fashion around the planets, a periwinkle-colored beam of energy always with ye. Ah am as old as the masters of the Dullahan. We have been opposing forces since the dawn of time. Ah am Galactic Magic incarnate."

No one said anything. Not even a snarky comment came from the children or Benji. All contemplated this statement. But Arthur was next to break the second moment of silence, "I don't understand. When did this happen?"

Moira nodded; Arthur was probably feeling betrayed seeing how close they were, "As ah've said, ah have always been the Galactic Magic incarnate. Of course, ah didn't know until quite recently. It began with a dream, one that kept me asleep for a long time. Ah had no idea what it was or what it wanted, but the magic within me pushed forward and made itself known. All ah had to do was choose who ah wanted to be. And like ye and yer brothers, I chose both too."

Skylar and her siblings nodded, starting to understand how cool this news was, "So, let's get to the real story. What can you do?"

Moira chuckled, "Everything ye can imagine, ah am not fixed to any planet or solar system, ah am everywhere. But, ah cannot stop the enemy. We might have won the battle, but we will never win the war."

"But we should at least try, right?" asked Markus.

"Right, there will always be battles to fight, whether in this solar system or in others. We must be vigilant. And speaking of other solar systems—" Moira started as she turned to an empty space on the grass.

With a wave of her hand, Danu appeared, free from her magical bindings. She plopped down onto the ground in a pathetic mess. Her hair was disheveled, and her dress had some dirt. A few chuckles rang throughout the crowd, but Moira silenced them all with a raised hand.

"Danu, its time ye answer for yer crimes," said Moira authoritatively.

Danu looked up at her. Her eyes widened in horror. She knew exactly what Moira had become and that her troubles were only beginning, "Please, have mercy!"

"Mercy? Like the mercy ye showed to the people of Avalon and the gods who rightfully rule these planets? Yer an intruder, Danu. Ye were never meant to rule this solar system. But there is one solar system missing its planet. And if ye leave now, ye might just be *their* hero," Moira said knowingly.

"I...I cannot return there. I was never loved, never worshiped. I was the planet they all ignored."

"Perhaps they have changed. A lot has happened there since ye left. Ye never know if ye don't go."

Danu found some courage hidden within herself as she replied, "No, I refuse to return."

Moira leaned down to Danu's level and whispered, "Danu, *ye* don't have a choice."

With a snap of her fingers, Danu turned into a ball of light, screaming as she was launched into the sky, disappearing from the solar system altogether. Cheers rang out through the crowd, all excited they didn't have to deal with her schemes anymore. Moira smiled at their happiness and peace and gave the boys the planet Danu once occupied, where they could create it how they deemed best. They'd be the guardians of the solar system. Although this planetary change might affect the others, all the gods would be prepared for it and come to an agreeable solution.

Macha had gone through enough trauma, and because the boys destroyed her planet, she no longer had a place to call home. But before she could even suggest it, Morrighan offered her home to her. It only made sense to Moira seeing their relationship. And their union wouldn't affect the planets nearly as much since their personalities were similar. As for the torture planet the Dullahan created for himself, Moira blasted the planet apart. She spread its remains across the solar system, creating a ring around the outermost planets. If the Dullahan's masters were to come back for more data, she'd use the magic from that planet against them. The solar system was officially impenetrable. But the same couldn't be said for the other solar systems and the other Earths out there. The enemy was out there still, but Moira was certain their unified cause would allow them to come to any planet's aid.

About the Author

Ceara Comeau hails from New Hampshire and has been writing for over a decade. Her writing career began with self-publishing collections of short stories which later turned into full length novels. Up until her early twenties, she had published six books. It was at this time that the young author dove into the world of science fantasy beginning a new adventure. It was then that she decided to take a series she worked hard on developing years ago and rewrite it. It first started out as an eight book novella series, then to a trilogy, and then it turned into one book, "Memories of Chronosalis". This book invites the reader to get a glimpse at one of the solar systems in the universe that she's creating. It also received the Pinnacle Book Achievement Award. Following this she wrote, "A Scientist's Remorse" which is a history of the characters introduced in "Memories of Chronosalis". In 2023, Ceara launched her film company called Book Sisters Productions where she dedicated her time to putting those stories onto the big screen.